MOSTLY TRUE STORIES

AND OTHER LIES

To Me - And like And is a few life - there wart's

Also by Roger G. Ritchey

**Hankering For The Way It Was—
Mostly true short stories**
(Dancing Moon Press, 2013)

Mostly True Stories And Other Lies

Roger G. Ritchey

DANCING MOON PRESS
NEWPORT, OREGON

MOSTLY TRUE STORIES AND OTHER LIES

copyright © Roger G. Ritchey, 2015
All rights reserved

Paperback ISBN: 978-1-937493 78-3
Ebook ISBN: 978-1-837493-79-0
Library of Congress Control Number: 2015931422

Ritchey, Roger G.
Mostly True Stories And Other Lies
1. Short stories-fiction; 2. Memoir; 3. Oregon History, early 20th century;
4. Forest Grove, Oregon; 5. Farm life in Oregon, early 20th century;
6. Humor. 7. Historical photos. I. TITLE

Cover image: Dwight L. McCue and his white Leghorn chickens (1930).
"The Mystery Mustang" (and two illustrations) excerpted from *Trail Dust: Sketches on the Trail* by W. Howard Hamm, 1950. Second printing, 1981.
"Th' Church In Th' Canyon," (and illustration) from *Trail Dust 2: Sketches on the Trail*, by W. Howard Hamm, 1981.
Excerpts from *Ever Westward*, by Bill Stucker, 1962. From Preface.
Excerpt from *The View From Where I Stand* by Richard L. Ramsell

Cover design & production: *Sarah Gayle and Wayne Plourde, SolaLuna Studios*
Book editing, design & production: *Carla Perry, Dancing Moon Press*
Manufactured in the United States of America

DANCING MOON PRESS

P.O. Box 832, Newport, OR 97365; 541-574-7708
www.dancingmoonpress.com
info@dancingmoonpress.com

FIRST PRINTING

Dedication

I dedicate this book to those who came before me. Each of us is a composite of all those happy chromosomes trying to get along. In my case, I'm fairly sure there's still a little Irish bickering taking place deep inside my core.

I also dedicate this book to several high school teachers. They busted their butts trying to convey helpful growing-up suggestions. These teachers include a very gentle lady, Miss Leone Graham, Mrs. Josephine Hunkapillar (who had an amazing capacity to keep my interest ratcheted), Mrs. Beatrice Bliss (who became a published author), Mr. John Paul Bennett (who taught me math like no other), Mrs. Catherine Dunn (who skillfully guided us in her speech class), and Mr. Arthur Brachman (whose patience was legendary). I take off all my many hats to their combined efforts to polish their products.

Contents

SECTION 2: Three To A Hill: A Tribute to Uncle Dwight McCue

SECTION 3: Stories, Poems, and Excerpts By My Family

Preface

The first section of this book contains stories that are mostly true, or could have happened. Some are on the lighter side and others slant in another direction, as all of us do sometime during our lives.

The photo on the cover of this book is of my uncle Dwight L. McCue—my mother's brother—and the story of his life is featured in Section 2 of this book. The cover image shows him holding two of his white Leghorn laying hens. Dwight grew up in St. Paul and New Ulm, Minnesota, but moved to Forest Grove, Oregon in 1927 to start a small farm. It was unusual back then for a man to be raised in town and then become a farmer. Usually, guys went from the farm to the city. Dwight's brothers predicted he would fail. Uncle Dwight was a man with immense capabilities, many of which were self-taught. And he was a hoot to be around. I've tried to follow his advice all my life and to emulate many of his habits. I've had a happier time because of it. "Three To A Hill" is Dwight's story.

This book concludes with Section 3—stories, poems, and illustrations by a few of my deceased relatives including W. Howard Hamm, Bill Stucker, and Richard L. Ramsell. Perhaps writing runs in families.

I am very interested in your reactions to these stories and poems and encourage direct feedback. Please write or call:

Roger G. Ritchey

3005 NE East Devils Lake Road, Otis, OR 97368

541-994-5739

rlakehs@charter.net

SECTION 1

**Mostly True Stories
And Other Lies**

The Trick

Sissit, sissit, sissit!

The well-used hot, stale air was happy to escape. I was more than happy to aid that tired air, let it get back with its own kind. Well, I was happy and dumb, really dumb. But that is the thing about dumb—you don't really know Stupid until later, sometimes much later.

I was halfway done with letting that recycled, pooped-out air out of the back tire on the cop's car in Hillsboro. It had started out as a prank and well… a little payback, too.

And the payback plan part could easily be described as a generous dose of stupid as well.

The Po-Leece had given me a warning the week before because of my 1955 Chevy's loud pipes. Their official language was Excessive Noise. I was pissed! The Irish part of me was acting out again. Truth be known, I should have been issued a ticket three or four months earlier, like most traffic tickets when you get them. But, I still like to think that I had the sweetest sounding pipes going, and most of the cops, well, they had been young once.

The nitty-gritty bottom line was I had ten—count 'em, ten—lousy days to remove my prized, beautiful Fenton

Headers. Neither I nor the car would ever be the same again! Their magnificent sound was both deep and rich. Sound carried a little better then, before all the neighborhood subdivisions, Walmarts and WinCos moved in. Those Fentons smacked your ears—even ole Grandpa's ears—more than a mile away, with a deeply satisfying, rumbling sound like rolling thunder coming down the valley. It was reminiscent of the movie classic, *Thunder Road*, with Robert Mitchum humming along, down the North Carolina back roads. And that was even without putting the gas pedal all the way down. And Lordy, Lordy… if you, could have heard them Fenton Headers in a tunnel, like on upper Burnside Street in Portland, why you'd think you were ripping through the Pearly Gates.

It was two a.m., the wee morning hours at the old Times Café in Hillsboro, across from the Washington County Courthouse. I knew the cop would park his ever-loving butt on his regular stool, eat limp French fries, and flirt with the bulging-topped waitress. She would respond to his lusty stare and to his always-generous tip. I was not sure which she liked the best. Hot, steaming, black coffee was going down too, and eventually going to help keep him awake—after his testosterone had cooled down.

There were still late night bar hangers-on going in and out of the Café and one of them might—in their soused up state—shoot off their mouth to the fuzz. But I gambled they did not enjoy his egotistical, hotshot personality any more than I did. And then, too, there was always the chance the cop would get a police phone call, hurrying him off of that warm stool and spoiling my fine surprise.

My stellar plan was to let air out of diagonal tires, virtually down to the rims. That was the "A" part, and then I would come roaring by with my soon-to-be-removed Fenton Headers bellowing one of their last nighttime songs. Hotshot would stop stuffing the French fries and staring at the Times entertainment for a little while. Letting him earn his paycheck, and letting me have a little fun was the "B" part.

The third "C" part of my plan plunked into place like a silver dollar in a slot machine. I realized I could not do the entire air letting out because Hotshot would know for sure that it was me setting him up.

So, who should come along, but a good high school chum slightly loaded with reliable Blitz beer. Bert Benson happily could and would be the chief air-letter-outer while I made sure I was seen inside the Times Café, seemingly sober, my insides energized by that piping hot, black stuff.

While all this was going down, the chilly night, *and* father time, *and* the Scottish part of me began emerging from my booze-induced addled brain and I started to comprehend the monster problem I was creating. I could end up in the Hillsboro hoosegow!

My persistent juvenile Irish dumbness noticed a dim light was beginning to come on.

And so plan "D" became... just leave Hotshot to his fries, coffee, and ogling, while he forever scratched his butt about the flat tire trick.

I did wonder what the regular Times Café crowd would say behind his back and what Hot Pants would tell the waitress with the hourglass figure.

A Mama's Boy?

So, okay, maybe it's true I was a mama's boy… for a bunch of reasons. One reason is that I used to help Mom iron clothes and I really enjoyed every little hot pressing stroke. Oh, I know they were just handkerchiefs or real simple items like pillowcases, but in my six-year-old brain, I was helping Mom. That was something that maybe God just programmed me to do. I also learned how to sew and so just maybe, I was a little sew & sew, too.

My sister, Carol, and I traded off on the dishes—one night I'd wash and she'd dry, and then we'd switch roles the next night. Back and forth. At first, I was too short to reach the sink or drying rack, so I'd stand on a small, eight-inch-high homemade wooden stool that could tip on you now and then. Somebody had painted it a glossy white and black. My guess is that the stool was handed down from my cousin, Dean Ritchey. I also used that stool in the bathroom to wash my hands, so it was well traveled and well used.

Mom was big time on being clean and orderly. I never ever saw a mess in her house. Shoot, I don't even recall dust settling on any surface.

I didn't learn how to cook, but I dang well should have, as that skill could have come in handy when I was in college. My two Oregon State University roomies—Tom Paterson and George McKibben, who I'd known since high school—poked fun at me each time I decided to tear home on a weekend. Part of my need was just to see Mom, who felt sorry for us college students in our deprived state. She'd cook up a big casserole dish and those roomies of mine sure slurped up her special vitals with big smiles on their faces. Okay, I have to admit that my roomies were both on their way to becoming pretty dang good chefs, and I was envious.

As a little kid, I spent a lot of time in the family garden with Mom because she'd haul me there in my little red wagon while I was still in diapers. Our garden was down by Carpenter Creek, a half-mile from the house because that location was handy to the irrigation water. The winding road was through a hog and cow pasture comprising about 25 acres. The original family garden was used by all three Ritchey brothers' families for a few years, then taken over by just my Aunt Bert and Uncle Paul (Dad's brother), and our family for many years after that. Mom would do some hand-weeding or hoeing, then load the wagon with vegetables—and, of course, with me—and back up the long hill we'd go with the big, old mama sows watching us, eyeballing their future scraps.

Those scraps provided another fun chore for me because as soon as I could carry a small pail with a few vegetable peelings, Mom would let me tag along to feed the sows. I remember having to change hands often to distribute the weight, and that the rim kept banging against my little legs. This neat morning chore with the sows happened every day except Sunday, when we got ready for church and a good sermon.

I think with a little training, you could get a pig to go into any church, and I'm pretty sure the denomination would not matter to the hog. It's possible that if pigs were allowed in, the level of intelligence of the parishioners would be elevated. And I figure that a pig in the front pew would sure enough get the preacher's attention—way more than when my Dad would fall asleep and then wake with a good snort. I can see the Forest Grove *News Times* headline—The Preacher and the Porker.

There'd always be a few of our 15 or 20 sows waiting, making smacking sounds and jockeying for the best spot, when Mom and I hauled out the scraps. We didn't use a trough because our scraps weren't watery. And they most definitely were not table leftovers, because nothing was ever left over from our meals. Those pig scraps were the cooked potato peelings or cornhusks, or other such waste. When those hogs would catch a hold of a tasty morsel, well, that's when you'd hear some real smacking. And bickering. And the showing of a tusk or two for dominance. And those tusks were sharp! After the excitement settled down, Mom would let me climb up to on the second board down and hold me as I leaned over to scratch their bristly backs. A pig's upper hide is tough and hard, not soft and pliable like a cow's upper hide. As I got a little older, sometimes I would jerk their curly tails, which just made them tuck them in tighter to their butts.

Speaking of curly tails, why do you suppose pigs have them? Just right off, I can't think of any other domestic animal that has a curly tail—not even wild ones!

Our barn and the first pasture were about a 150 yards north of our home. This fenced pasture had a large steel-framed gate and a short wooden panel adjacent that was easy to climb or hop over. As I got older, I'd run up and put one hand on the panel to help me leap over the fence in my unrepentant youth. As I think back, those oinkers had it pretty good on our farm, in addition to the daily routine of morning scraps. There was all the green pasture they could eat, grain once a day, a creek to drink out of, and a dry and clean barn that they shared with the steers.

I had it pretty good, too, because that's the way it was on a family farm for a mama's boy in western Oregon during the 1940s.

I Love Pockets

Pockets: A Boy's Take

I used to have full pockets. Just the changing of my pants was a job, but a super fun job. I once was almost Huck Finn, but then I changed… was that good? I never knew anybody else named Huck—maybe the name comes from Huckster. It might not be a nice name to have given the fun some kids have with names—me included. Huck could have grown up like the kid in Johnny Cash's song, "A boy Named Sue."

I am not sure when I first became aware of how incredibly neat pockets are. It was probably when wearing baby pajamas with pockets in the late 1930s. Even now, I can remember how handy they were for storing my pacifier.

Soon after, my pockets held a piece of gum, a marble, hard candy, and a nickel. The list of objects I could fit in there just kept growing. You can never have too much, is what I used to think.

Then for years and years, my absolute prize was a Case pocketknife with two blades. The knife somehow opened a whole new world to me—I had become a real somebody. I religiously cleaned that knife, rechecked for dirt and rust,

ROGER G. RITCHEY

and *always* had one blade shaving sharp. The other blade I used for scraping and such.

Whenever I jammed my hands all the way down into my pockets, I would take inventory. I would feel each special treasure and rub it. Having a morning ritual is important and besides, inventories are good practice. It was important to make sure there were no holes in my pants, from which I could lose my prized possessions. One can take this checking your goodies too far, however, especially doing that rubbing thing.

I have thought long and hard about the advantages of being part kangaroo, or even a female possum, because pockets and money belts are patterned after standard marsupial equipment. There would be this giant built-in pocket that would never get a hole in it. I'm not sure how you'd wash it though, because all pockets collect special crud—lint, woodchips, body fuzz, gum wrappers. You'd have a giant belly button in your pocket, manufacturing who knows what. I think my Levi pants pockets turn inside out when they are too weighted down with gunk and maybe kangaroos take a header in the water now and then for the same reason.

I used to always have full pockets and just the changing of my pants was a job. But I learned to empty those pockets before Mom did the Monday wash. Yes, sir, it was set in stone—Monday was washday. It was an

22

absolute gonna happen, like church every Sunday. Back then, cleanliness used to be next to Godliness except, like a lot of other things, that changed.

Here's a fact—Juicy Fruit gum does not make a happy camper in your pocket when it is slopping around in your mother's washtub and handwringers. I definitely noticed Mom was always extra careful when running my clothes through that stuff, and praise her now for showing more common sense than most folks. And I still vividly recall seeing Mom hanging the laundry on the outside clotheslines and hearing them snap in the wind. Those sun and wind-dried clothes always had a fresh air smell. It was hard for her to switch to an electric dryer when we got one of those. I still have her old wooden clothespins hanging around.

Another really swell feature about pockets is that they keep your hands warm. My Minnesota grandpa, Mac McCue, told me about carrying a hot, oven-baked potato in his pocket when trudging to work in the wintertime. Good pockets can even eliminate the need for mittens, since at least one mitten is always trying to get lost.

Perhaps most important in the world of pockets is that at the frisky age of twelve or so, one can look really cool and hip! Having both hands thrust deep in your pockets will make you appear nonchalant and give you that James Dean and Steve McQueen look.

Pockets: A Slightly More Mature Kid's Take

Now I carry what I laughingly refer to as "my brains" inside my pocket. I'm referring to a small notebook that supposedly helps me remember. Naturally, a notebook requires a ballpoint pen, and I like to have a pencil handy, too. Generally, there is usually at least one business card in my pocket, along with some special papers. I save these precious "brain" books, God knows what for, and some of them are going on fifty years old. They've grown several layers of Oregon's own special mold and algae. I know my wife thinks I'm some dysfunctional ding-a-ling.

You probably think I've just been talking about pants and overall pockets. Oh, no! I never buy a shirt without pockets. Notice that I used the plural word "pockets," because one lonely pocket doesn't cut it. And I do not mean half-deep golfers dumb show pockets. I'm talking about deep pockets you can put something worthwhile in, and ensure it won't fall out. Now focus on that word "deep" because you will be quizzed later, especially you of the so-called weaker sex.

Naturally, buttons—or preferably flaps with buttons—snug down your treasures and keep them real tidy. I find it downright disgusting when I bend over and have everything, including my brains spill out. The worst is when bending over the commode wearing clothes made with ill-conceived shirt pocket imitations. Toilet fishing has to be done real quick, 'cause wringing pee-water out of a brain book is not fun.

It's important to mention new travel clothes. Travel clothes have pockets inside of pockets, in places one would never guess or want to guess. Some even have Velcro covers and are zippered, too. The Velcro covers make a ripping noise as you pull them apart, letting you know when somebody is after your goodies.

Pockets: An Adult's Take

Now, if you are lucky enough to have deep pockets then please listen up here! It is especially important that you women are let in on this timely economic lesson. I will tell you why there are many more men billionaires than women. We men are inclined—or at the very least pre-programmed—about pockets. The astute reader will remember that I previously alluded to deep pockets. The term was not used just for the heck of it. There are multiple subtle implications about deep pockets, all of which you women can hopefully grasp.

I know women are always sucking up to Warren Buffet, but the women never try to emulate him. They are just trying to get some of what he's got, and anticipating a real buffet. It is obvious having your own private Mr. Buffet is way better than winning the lottery, and he just keeps making more of what he's got enough of. It's almost like he prints money, whether he needs it or not. Well not only Buffet, but Bill Gates, Mr. Google, that Apple Guy, and the Feds. I strongly suspect there are a lot of women who wish Mr. Buffet were a Mormon fellow with an affinity for several wives, or maybe they're hoping to land one of those oil guys who need a wife harem.

Here's where I go out on a long, spindly limb, but it appears to me that purses are a pain in the patootie. Women are always shuffling their purses, first in front, then over the shoulder, or around their neck. This shuffling consumes a lot of energy, energy that could be spent getting deep pockets. I've said it now, exposed myself, for who knows what. But financial truth has a cutting edge, ringing deep and loud, like an old time cash register, one that flashed the numbers up for both sides to see and so you know you are not being cheated. Of course, now-a-day's women are constantly losing stuff in their big, fat purses, so naturally it's "dig" or "dump." What a time waster!

I'm sure we all remember what the reliable Ben Franklin said about time and money. Time is Money. T=$. The equation seems relatively simple, doesn't it?

Then there's all the creeps who steal—you guessed it—a women's purse. In the old days, when pickpockets were slick, they grabbed your money on the sly. Now women are likely to get their necks broke when their purse strap is yanked from around their throats. Even being slick has become obsolete and the pickpockets have morphed into dangerous thieving creeps.

I suggest that bib overalls might be the cat's meow to stop this rash of purse stealing. And bibbies are God's answer to not being born a kangaroo. I guess we could give women a choice—be born again as a kangaroo, or wear bibbies. I would wager there would be a substantial increase in wealthy women going the bibbie route, but on the other hand, we might become overpopulated with kangaroos.

I need to point out right here that there are many positive reasons for wearing bibbies. First, bib overalls have very adequate gaps in the side for cooling, not to mention scratching some bothersome itch—and even those in high society have to scratch sometimes. Also, bibbies stay up without requiring an uncomfortable belt, and just as importantly, there's no chance of a butt crack being exposed while bending over. Although some of you buxom babes may want to wear a t-shirt on top. By the way, did any of you know that t-shirt is simply an abbreviation for tit-shirt? Check it out in Ritchey's Dictionary, on page three-ninety-sex.

Have I got you convinced about bibbies yet? If not, just wait a sec for this next idea. Think about the advantages of bibbies when nursing a baby. I've read where bib overalls are fashionably popular with women who've had twins. I know, I know, I should not have started down this path, but I'm truly trying to help and get genuine equality for both genders, if that is possible.

I'm hoping to convince female readers of two things— First, purchase pants and shirts or blouses only if they have deep, quality pockets. Second, women should give full consideration to including those liberating bibbies in their wardrobe. Hmmm, I think I'll start coloring some bib overalls in a sexy, hot-pink color and become a fake Irish-Italian clothes designer.

So, in summary, if you have big, deep pockets, or if you wear bib overalls, you'll have bushels of room to pack around your brains, which is a significant contributor to creating real deep financial pockets.

Wanting and Waiting

Did you ever suffer from the *I wants*? Boy, I sure did! My story starts in 1951. No, it actually started back in 1947. That's when I got my first bicycle, which was quite a step up from a tricycle. You can probably recall your own trauma going from three kind-of-steady tricycle wheels down to just two. Dad brought home a new bike as a surprise for me. He was great for surprises.

But I did not want my first bicycle. And not because it was a kid's half-bike, a learner. I guess I was just being stubborn—an obnoxious trait that often goes with the territory at the age of seven. Or maybe I was stretching out the terrible twos. In any case, the bike had been just where I set it for least a month, and to my folks' disappointment, I still did not know how to ride it. I hadn't even tried to learn, other than a few halfhearted wobbly wrecks.

Then Mom and Dad played a trick on me—a mean trick. I loved to go with my dad to the main farm and on drives in his truck wherever he went. A dreadfully harsh sentence was imposed when my mom said, "You can't go with your dad anywhere until you learn to ride your bicycle." Mom and Dad sure knew how to make me say "uncle."

Well, I learned how to ride—backwards, no hands, hanging off the side, and every which way. So I showed them! I have to admit that my sometimes-mean big sister was a great help as I initially learned to balance myself. But she never did diddly for me unless good things were coming her way. I suppose Mom bribed her with extra helpings of yummy homemade chocolate pudding topped with our own cow cream.

Then guess what happened!

Yes, siree! I outgrew that little bike, almost before you could say Jack Robinson. (I've always wondered if the saying was about the Jackie Robinson of baseball fame, 'cause that guy—old number 42—was faster than greased lightning.) In my nightmares, I would conjure the image of a basketball player on a runt's bicycle. You know the bike is too small when your pumping knees hit your jaw, or when you thrust your knees outward, but both positions are ridiculous. I'd been getting funny looks from the other kids, and there probably was some whispering behind my back. I decided I could wait no longer and still maintain my proper place in our hick gang's pecking order.

So I opened negotiations to get a grownup bicycle. The talking went on forever. I *had to have* a bike more fitting for a twelve year old.

The looking began, just pictures to peruse, or demonstration models to try out, because—can you believe it—no, as in zero, bikes were in stock. Finally, two lifetimes later, we ordered a bike from Miller's Ace Hardware Store. Then the *real* wait began. I thought the Ohio bicycle factory must have been mining the ore for the frame and planting the rubber trees for the tires. I began harboring a grudge against the whole state of Ohio.

I pestered my mom until she was sick of listening to me whine. "When will it get here?" "What's taking so long?" "Why doesn't it come?"

I would get all sweaty just thinking about that shiny red bike. I simply *could not wait* until that bicycle was delivered. I even went to sleep at night dreaming about my new wheels. Boy was I going to be the *cock of the walk*.

The big day finally arrived and there it was—brand spanking new—just waiting for me to jump on. The nice guys at the hardware store had already assembled it. (I think those old Ace Hardware duffers had been kids once, too.) Also, Mom might have pushed a button or two at Ace because Dad had already been gone for two years and she didn't want to do the assembling.

So... no hesitation now. I just jumped on that sucker and flew down Stringtown, Dilley, and Ritchey Roads, which had been asphalt-paved in the prior few years. Naturally, I had to parade my new wheels to anybody who cared to look, or want to touch this long-sought prize.

It took me a long time to understand (maybe I'm a tad

slow on the uptake), but I never did love that red bicycle nearly as much as I did my first little kid's bike. One of life's bittersweet lessons about all those desperate "I wants" is that now, at the age of seventy-five, I look back and realize that more than a few of them turned out to be just a white elephant.

The Flying Machine

My first attempts
Were rather crude
And blunt of nose
As beginnings usually are
Then I honed my skill
Boeing aerodynamics
Was my aim

Soon I had a model
Of a paper airplane
That fit the game

Why, even Mom
Was impressed
And it took a lot of moxie
To make her Irish
Blue-green eyes shine

My third-generation try
Made from her used typing paper
Zipped and zagged
Then looped before it dove
Straight at the ground

One of my trials
Nosedived straight into
Mom's banana cream pie

I kept a straight face
Sis laughed up the place
Both the cats
Wanted to play
But the smarter dog
Who had more savvy
Growled, *Don't make me stay*

It was all harmless fun
Unless I zoomed in
To someone's eye
Oh, I'm just testing
Your reactions
Was what I would cry!

The *HOT* One

I vividly remember having my butt up against her. My affair had started a long time before that. She was so warm, and it felt sooo, sooo good! And I knew from many previous experiences just how good she felt. It would go on for hours—I only had to "prime" her occasionally.

We were a matched pair although she was a lot older than me. Actually, she was what some folks call an old school marm, and that's where I first found her. She was larger than me, too, close to six feet tall and rather broad across the beam, but pleasingly so. My only complaint was that sometimes she got too hot, but pure and simple, she had the hots for me!

I loved her sounds too, because I have a strong need to communicate. Sometimes this facet of my personality is nearly overpowering, especially in the early morning hours after a chilly night. Oh, we didn't touch much. Somehow, she wasn't into that kind of intimacy. Occasionally, I would reach out, but at least twice, I regretted that gesture.

I never did know how old she was because she acted so young. I haven't seen her in thirty years, but man, I sure think about her.

Now, in my later life, I really need to tell it like it was and finally get all this off my chest. I'm ready to let my whole family know, although I'm sure some had guessed about our intimate relationship.

Even today, nothing can compare to that old upright woodstove on the family farm, the one that came out of the old three-room Dilley School.

I wonder if she is still keeping things hot.

The Mercy Killing

Raw, stark, brutality was the way of real farm life in the 1940s and 1950s when I grew up. Today, our society has an almost insane desire for TV reality shows, which is merely selective reality of course… as in turning the remote power button on and off. Well, I had ample doses of real life during my adolescence—enough to last several lifetimes.

I'm about to relate the story of a terrible event exactly the way it happened many years ago, and I understand if some of you choose to stop reading here and move on to the next story.

I certainly wanted to leave the traumatic scene, but escaping was not an option. I still desire to remove myself mentally, even now, after the sixty years have passed. *All*, as in each one of us, are burdened by our memories. Sometimes we get lucky and manage to forget something along the way, but this is one burden that has stuck.

In my middle teens, I was larger than many of my schoolmates, but not quite a grown man. However, on the Richter scale for reality and hard life experiences, I may have been an old geezer compared to my classmates.

The two main reasons for this fake maturity were the

family time bombs that had already been ticking. First, my dad and grandfather died within two weeks of each other, when I was ten years old. A weight—strangely both hated *and* desired—was placed upon me and it changed me forever. *You are the man of the house,* was a phrase I heard innumerable times, but only a tiny portion of me wanted to be a man, and only during delusional macho moments.

Second, and more deeply interwoven, Dad had farmed with his two younger brothers. Most partnerships do not survive, but this one flourished even though there were always undercurrents welling up. The muted inter-family rivalries (primarily among the three wives) became more apparent after my dad passed away. Or maybe I matured sufficiently to become more cognizant of the layered and octopus-like complexities. All of this family stuff piled weight upon me to act like a man at that tender young age. Only a minute part of me was ready for this giant step into adulthood.

The family joining had resulted in a larger land base than most farm operations in western Oregon. There is always a percentage of agricultural land that can't be cultivated—due to creeks, wetlands, steep terrain, and bad soil. This lower class land is often devoted to pasture or to timber. I would guess our pasture and woodlands property exceeded two hundred acres. Consequently, counting all types of livestock, our annual animal numbers could exceed six or seven hundred head. Then, mathematically it is a given, there will be animal problems every year.

Most livestock "situations" were routine and mundane, although I suppose a city kid might assume some days were rodeo fun. NOT this day! This horrible, anguished animal trauma rose abruptly one late summer day.

Our standard practice for emasculating bull calves back then was done using a device with a crazy French name, Burdizzo. Even the name sounds cruel. I've always regarded this tool as primitive—probably a leftover from the Inquisition or Dark Ages. The device is shaped like a heavy pruner with medium-length handles. The extra-broad jaws are approximately three inches. They did not cut, but used a severe crimping action on a bull's testicle cord.

I do not know how animal pain compares to humans, but all of us—man or woman—know the reproductive area is tender and easily injured. Every year on our farm, three or four hundred animal castrations were necessary. And we often did our own dogs and cats, plus cut the dog's tail off on certain breeds. Pig's ears were routinely notched for identification purposes, and bulls usually had a big copper nose ring to help maintain control of the two thousand pound beasts.

We had somehow missed one bull calf, which by then was about ten months old. The jaws of the Burdizzo must have been placed on the wrong spot when we finally got him in the cattle chute and applied the crimper. This horrible error resulted in constricting his ability to urinate and he bloated terribly from the toxic fluid buildup. The bloating rapidly became excruciating pain for the bull and he bellowed and bawled far into the night.

The next morning, one uncle grabbed me to help kill the young bull. We took a heavy sledgehammer, which was commonly used for killing animals in slaughterhouses during those archaic times. Another uncle, the one who normally did the killing of animals with a .30/30 rifle for our own family's butchering, was away on business.

I'm pretty sure my uncle latched onto me rather than his own older son because my mental psyche was tougher, or at least I was macho dumb enough to project the image of being tougher. Perhaps I was more resilient, or lucky enough to be a teenage survivor, but the front I wore was a false one. I think we all construct moats in our minds as a form of preserving our sanity. But my moat was about to go into overload.

The young bull was standing in a pasture down near Carpenter Creek. He made no attempt to evade us. Maybe all the inflammation locked his joints and he could not run.

First, my uncle visually measured the distance, and then took several hearty whacks at the bull with the sledgehammer. He was skilled with these kinds of hand tools and it was obvious that he had grown up with axes and mauls. Most folks can't hit the mark with much consistency, including me at that age. This missing the mark is why those showoff studs at county fairs almost always fail when attempting to clang the bell and win the prize for their cutie-pie.

However, the overhead swinging motion was more difficult than usual because the height of the animal's head was nearly breast high, which severely compounded our leverage problem. Slaughterhouse killing is normally accomplished with one blow at the bottom of the swing.

The bull did not budge, even after my uncle had hit him several times. He just bawled and bellowed louder and louder. The sound was terrible to hear and smell and feel!

My uncle gave the sledge up to me. I tried my sixteen-year-old best, but achieved exactly the same results, nothing positive to put the poor animal out of his misery. I tried to shut out everything and bury the horrible incident many layers deep, but his calls echoed and re-echoed through my young mind. I learned much later that I had not shoved the memory far enough back into my closet and now, I often think about the increased pain of that stricken animal. Several years later, I talked with a slaughter guy who said it is imperative to achieve the kill on the first or second blow, and the spot is very critical.

The bull was still standing. My uncle and I were

panting heavily from our exertion and the sick animal kept standing there, pleading with his eyes. Animal eyes in pain or fright have always bothered me immensely, which is the biggest reason I never took up deer or elk hunting.

There wasn't anything else to do, so we continued at our horrible task. The top of the bull's skull soon turned to mush and gore, splattering us each time we hit. It was indescribably awful even though I was preconditioned to death through too many other animal chores. The young, six-hundred-pound animal never moved. It was as if his joints were set in stone.

We finally realized sledging was not going to do it. My uncle said, 'Do you have a knife?' I responded, 'Yes, but only a small one.'

My uncle reluctantly drew out a larger knife from his pocket, but it was abnormally dull—he was a man who always kept his tools sharp. It turned out he had lost his old knife and this brand new one was like a hoe used in a rock quarry. I thought I heard him curse and mumble, 'It's brand new and not sharpened.' (I never figured out why the Case Knives were not proud enough to pre-sharpen their new pocketknives.)

We attempted to cut the bull's throat, but cattle have a lot of thick, folded hide located there. It's called a dewlap, which has multiple skin layers, and perhaps that helps protect cattle's jugular veins from carnivores.

We sawed and sawed with that new, dull knife and finally got far enough in to reach his windpipe, then his jugular. That portion of his anatomy was much larger and tougher than I expected. The hot, red blood spurted out all over us, drenching our belly and legs.

The suffering animal continued to remain standing and ever so slowly bled to death, finally toppling over. I suppose the whole ordeal lasted thirty minutes or more. A half-hour of pure hell.

My uncle and I were feeling, smelling, and looking awful, just terrible, but like many loathsome farm jobs, it *simply had to be done.*

My purpose in sharing this story is that I hope the telling of it will relieve me of some of the nightmare memories.

The Wild Bunch

One little guy darted out to quick grab the pan of farm fresh cow's milk, then like lightening, zipped back under Mom's old chicken house. I could hear their vixen mother growling, scolding it for—I assume—getting too close to dreaded man.

There were five small gray streaks of high-octane energy and they had been whelped in early spring under our abandoned chicken house. It's possible the yummy smell of chicken still lingered for their ultra-sensitive noses and they wanted to be close to that hen house.

This happening took place in the late 1960s, after I had graduated from Oregon State University's Agriculture School in 1963 and was back living at home.

I had seen the sharp pointed ears of the mama fox several times—she was naturally super skittish too. For sure, kits are born shy and consider man an enemy. And our country-oriented society wasn't that many years past the five-dollar bounty paid for their silky-soft ears delivered to some County government authority. This was just another idiotic government plan that probably did not have a chance to pan out.

I fed the little guys for several weeks—against the objections of my pheasant-hunting uncle, Curtis Ritchey. And naturally, my mom wondered about my sanity, but she wasn't the first who'd had that thought, nor was that the first time that thought had crossed her mind.

We used to have quite a few red foxes, too, and they were sure pretty with their partially white bushy tails. The red foxes seemed to disappear about the same time as all the beautiful China pheasants and the quail. This was after some idiot brought possums to Oregon. Possums love eggs and they destroyed too many nests. Less bushy fence rows contributed to the losses as well.

I never named those little gray streaks—they were just a too-brief wildlife enjoyment. But I hope I helped them to survive.

The "Udder" Society

My cold fingers closed gently and I fondled her large, warm tits. Then I slowly squeezed on the upper section and her swollen mammary system began dripping milk.

Hand milking a cow starts with the index finger gradually closing on your palm. Then your middle finger, ring finger, and pinkie replicate the same movement in a simultaneous, fluid motion, forcing the milk downward and out of the spigot-teat.

Most of the farm kids I knew hated the dismal thought of milking cows! But I loved it!

I distinctly remember learning how to milk, and I'd like you to keep in mind that it's hard to get the hang of it on the first go around, so it's best to start with a gentle cow. And a warning—Bovines *do not* enjoy milkers with long fingernails, or irritated folks who grind their teeth. In fact, I've never known an uptight dairyman because cows enjoy—and ultimately demand—both calmness and contentment while they are being milked.

Another chore I really loved was fetching our small milking herd from the lower pasture down by the creek. Of course, half the time my cousins and I were sent on this daily mission just to get us out of what was left of our parents' hair. But the trek to the creek always included a new adventure, and oftentimes even funner things just happened to happen.

There was a swamp near the creek with huge clumps of reed canary grass and it was a game to see if we could jump from one clump to another without falling in the murky water. I was almost eighteen months older than my cousin Gary Ritchey, and I noticed he had this affinity to get his pants wet whenever we were within a quarter mile of a drop of water. So, to help him out, I'd pick grass clumps in the swamp that were a long way apart. His getting soaked regularly earned him a lively swat or two from his mom. But I guess the swats weren't hard enough to keep him from clump jumping the very next afternoon.

That daggone swamp water was like a magnet! Mallard ducklings often hid in these grass mounds and they'd go skittering off after their quacking mom. Of course, my cousin, Gary, and I would be glued right onto their stubby pin-feathered tails. And, if the dogs were along, there'd be a merry chase. Sometimes the cows would be grazing in the swamp, but they were ready to leave with promise of ground grain.

More fun happened down the quarter-mile lane along which we had to drive the cows. Cow-critters tend to walk in paths behind the leader, so following their trail meant we had to dodge fresh cow pies and try to trick each other into stepping in one.

We could always tell if it was going to rain, 'cause the cows would get all excited and almost gallop causing their udders to swing wildly from side to side. It didn't take long to learn that the higher their tails went in the air, the sooner and more it would rain. I think animals are more sensitive to barometric pressures than us so-called "smarter" homosapiens, but sometimes we could smell the rain coming too. Rain usually came gently down the Gales Creek valley.

Our milk cows were a breed called Milking Shorthorns, which we crossed with a White Face—our King Bull—that had curls on his massive forehead and a big copper ring inserted in his nose. His highness's mighty hoofs stomped and pawed the earth, and wasn't he proud!

Shorthorns are medium-to-large size and were developed to provide farm families with both milk and beef. These cows have a vast array of color patterns and our most unusual cow was a mottled white on black. Her actual color came out like a blue roan. She was beautiful! *She knew it, too!* She was a natural for being the "boss cow."

Anyway, by evening, the cows were always ready for us to herd them up to the barn. They wanted the yummy ground grain, and they needed to be milked, especially if they had recently calved. When my cousin and I would reach the barn, the cows would file in to their own personal stalls. The blue boss cow was generally the first one in. That order rarely changed because the cows were self-sorting, like chickens with their pecking system. Unless we forgot, my cousin and I would pour out their feed before we headed down to the pasture. If we forgot to prepare the feed, the cows would stamp their hoofs, look around, and let us know with a moo or two!

Once the cows were secure in their stalls, I'd grab our Norwegian-made milk stool—not the three-legged jobbie kind that most farm movies depict. Our stools resembled a small box that had a two-foot-long by six-inch-wide tongue projecting out at a 15-degree angle on which to set the bucket. I still remain convinced that ours was a better "mousetrap" even after patiently listening to all those dumb knee-slapping, Swedish/Norwegian jokes. Our milk stool had been crafted by two second-generation Norwegian hired men, and it was the best because it was more stable.

Okay, next came the fun part—sitting down and slowly grabbing hold of the back tits, which typically contained the most milk. And I'll let you in on the secrets of successful cow milking…with your head nestled against the cow's flank, gradually work up to a steady squirt, squirt, squirt rhythm. The first few squirts are loud and tinny until the bottom of the bucket is coated with milk, which is when the squirt sound changes to a soothing slurp, slurp, slurp, rhythm. When a cow first freshens (gives birth to a calf and starts producing milk), she may give three or more gallons per milking. This amount of milk gradually decreases, but even after several months, there's still a lot of slurping.

As you milk along at a rapid pace and fill the pail, the warm milk starts to foam, building a bubbly froth. This foaming action helps intensify the distinctive odor of the fresh, warm milk. Many people find that aroma very pleasant and nurturing—perhaps it's a reminder of when we nursed as babies.

Sassy barn cats would make their appearance during milking to get a free shot or two. A full udder and teat can easily squirt eight or ten feet. So, occasionally, us kids would completely drench the cats, which gave them a half-hour licking job. But I never heard those fat cats complain.

Finishing, or stripping the cow properly, is critical. If you leave milk in the udder, the cows develop a disease called mastitis. This disease can affect just one teat or quarter, or all four, and the milk will develop a disturbing taste. Actually, it's just plain awful! And unmarketable—an entire ten-gallon can will be rejected.

In fairness, I must warn about the dangers of cow milking. One danger is a shit-covered tail switching at flies or, worse yet, at your not-so-happy face! Another is that a cow might start stomping her back hoof if you—or anything—ticks her off. For instance, cows don't like dogs running in front of their stalls and they'll often raise a foot and kick you right off of that well-made Norwegian stool in protest! Every now and then, a cow will get her hoof in the bucket, which makes every part of hell break loose. The sound and ruckus of a hoof in a clanking bucket is horrendous, and the chaos will disturb the other—usually placid—cows. But that's when those lucky barn cats fare pretty good as the recipients of all that dirty, ruined milk!

Our cows were normally kept indoors during the winter months. The pasture ground was simply too soft and, of course, the grass was not growing. In the spring, when we first turned the herd out on the pasture, they were like school kids on their first recess. They frolicked like young calves and their sheer joy was exhilarating to observe. And naturally, the happy cows over-ate the luscious green grass. You probably can guess what happens when that occurs. Lesson number 1 (which I learned very early, and it only took one time): don't stand behind a cow on new grass. Lesson number 2: watch where you step!

If you milk cows on a regular basis, you learn to become one with the cow. And becoming one with the cow allows your mind to go to other places. Time truly stands still and you become totally immersed in the moment. I cannot tell you how long it takes to milk a cow because I enjoyed myself so much. Time is meaningless. Besides, nobody had a wristwatch back then, and nobody was timing me. Milking cows is calming and relaxing when you get in a groove. I was grooving and groovy—way ahead of my time!

Another fun thing with cows is letting the calves suck on a mom. We typically had up to three calves of nursing age, and those calves would come shooting out of their nearby pen like hogs in a chute. We'd designate one cow as the "calf-cow" and after a year or two of vigorous sucking, the calf-cow's tits would angle outwards to accommodate those "starving" babies. Maybe that was a Darwinian thing happening right before our eyes.

It's hard to believe, but not everyone loves milking cows. During the early 1950s, we had a hot-tempered hired man from Arkansas helping us out. He was a tall dude, six-foot-three of sinewy muscle, and skinnier than a racing greyhound. One spring evening, this Arkansas dude got upset with a fresh heifer cow that didn't know the ropes and he jabbed her with a pitchfork. Twice! Me, being a sensitive kid, hated him for that act, and I immediately acquired a dislike for all things from that sorry southern state. That Arkansas a-hole nearly got fired over that jab.

After all the milking was finished, we'd strain the liquid into ten-gallon milk cans and place them in the cool milk house. This small adjacent structure had an enclosed concrete trough filled with cold water to preserve the milk for the local co-op's daily pickup. And everyday we'd bring a gallon of non-pasteurized milk home for our family's consumption. Mom would skim the cream off after the milk had chilled and risen to the top.

Then—more milk and cream fun! Us kids were always more than ready for some of our own genuine lip smacking. Mom's yummy double-batch chocolate or butterscotch pudding, tapioca, and sometimes even raisin-bread pudding filled the bill and everybody's tummy too. The *first* spoonful, down to the *last* spoonful, of homemade chocolate pudding covered with real cream is incredibly delicious!

I wish I had a big bowl full right now!

In conclusion, I simply have to thank the Udder Society for helping me discover that wonderful product—Bag Balm. Every barn had some on hand. This gooey stuff came in a distinctive green square can and is over-the-top-good for healing animal sores, chapped hands, and well, just about everything! I even read the other day that today's pro-golfers are regular users.

Another World

One of my most favorite activities is to lie under a large tree and gaze skyward. This ninety-degree shift in view easily transports me back to growing up on our western Oregon family farm. I can't go back as far as Alley Oop (from the funny papers), but as a kid I did have a Tom Sawyer mindset—and an insatiable desire to climb trees and build tree houses.

Recently, I went back to visit a special Douglas fir that for us kids was Mt. Everest. The tree is located 150 feet up the hill from a small stream that my cousin, Gary, and I could jump across—most of the time—in the summer. Thankfully, sixty years later, the tree survives. It has outlived beetles, wind, fire, lightning, and most surprisingly, man's destructive chainsaw.

That old matriarch was ancient back when I was young, evidenced by the gauged, craggy, rough bark and its gigantic stature. That magnificent tree is a relic of what we consider "old growth," and must be the grandmother of all the surrounding forest because its width and height dominate all the other trees nearby. The tree's lateral limbs are larger than the breast-high width of most of its far-flung progeny. The mossy but climbable limbs stair-step up in a slightly irregular pattern that provided just challenge enough for two ten-year-old adventuresome boys.

The view from halfway up—about 75 feet—made us feel like pirates on a ship's mast, especially on a breezy day. And the mostly gentle sway of the tree both soothed and stimulated us, encouraging our thoughts to be as untamed as the wind. We would take along a snack in order to linger later, because time did not matter—an hour became a minute. For us, Father Time did not exist!

The giant tree was situated halfway between Gary's house and my farm home—a perfect spot far enough away from both so that we couldn't be hollered home. It was not for us to be bothered by moms when there was a creek full of crawdads to check out. Back then, only our tummies were our timekeepers, and we knew supper would be waiting. Of course, the happy sun made its reliable arch, so we did have some idea about the hours passing.

My cousin, Gary, and I figured that this tree needed a platform because even though large, the limbs were still not big enough for us to safely take a little snooze. So, we began pulling boards up to secure a bird-like perch, which turned out to be a daunting task. We tried to enlist a neighborhood chum, David Alexander, who was younger than me, but several months older than Gary. But David was not a climber. He took one look at the mighty towering fir and stated, "You need to get another pirate." No amount of bribery or name-calling dented his skin. I even told David he could ride my bike—but no amount of sweet-talking worked on him either.

So, the humongous job was back on the two of us. Well, for sure, we wouldn't have to share our future house, and we didn't need to worry about the other kids attacking us. We'd pelt them with cones and, as a last resort, there was always that bathroom business—like knights did in the old timey castles.

Pulling those boards up, over, and around those grouse ladder limbs required genuine Herculean effort. With used nails stuffed in our pockets and the hammer through a loop on our pants, one of us would balance the board on a resting spot while the other climbed to the next pull-up spot, both of us grunting and straining for all we were worth. Finally, we tugged and toted the heavy rough-sawn two-by-sixes onto two nearly level limbs that had a narrow peek to the west of tree-lined Carpenter Creek.

After we caught our breath, I tried to nail the prize board down, but that old stick of wood was sun-dried and rock-hard. My first two attempts ended up with bent nails and a sore thumb, so that pirate part of me needed a break. Luckily, we had a couple of peanut butter and jelly sandwiches to go along with a big juicy Gravenstein apple out of Grandma Ritchey's special orchard.

Then Gary and I climbed down and went to the main barn to fetch some stout twine to hold down the board until a better plan came tearing along. But by then, we'd about had our fill of scampering around on limbs for one day—even on a dream tree made for climbing.

The tree was a favorite for the coons too, because we'd see their fresh claw marks and often got a whiff of their cherry-pit poop. Sometimes we'd spy a coon's tail drooping over a limb as he tried to sleep through our shenanigans, but generally, we had our homemade, maple-crotch slingshots handy and liked to lob a nut or two at them.

Some days, the neighborhood crows owned the treetop with their raucous behavior and the scads of different sounds they could make. Occasionally, a hunting red-tailed hawk's cry would split the deep silence of the woods.

The forest nearby was mostly fir but there were a few oaks and wild hazelnut trees too. In the fall, the squirrels would try and latch onto every nut the blue jays squawk-jabbered about. During the years when the acorn crop was heavy, us kids would watch our sow hogs in their happy grunting search, chomping on the oak trees' fall bounty.

Those days were a farm kid's ideal life. There was just no end to where our free and wild imaginations could take us.

A "Tom" And "Huck" Place

My younger cousin, Gary, and I had two Tom Sawyer and Huck Finn special places. The first was the tree house he and I built in a majestic old fir that I described in the story titled, "Another World."

Our second special place, "The Fort," was right next to Carpenter Creek, but we had to share it with the fat hogs. The spot was definitely more theirs then ours, because the pigs had built it. Most folks don't think porkers are thinking beasts with the ability to remember, but the truth is that they are flat-out smart. Pigs have an I.Q. similar to dogs. And I recently saw a canine on television that could identify several hundred objects without ever missing one. And that Eisenstein mutt was still learning.

Fat hogs are the ones heading for market, not used for breeding. Their weight ranged from twenty pounds just after they were weaned, to over two hundred pounds when they were ready for market and about to become bacon-burgers. The rapid weight gain happened in less than six months, especially if us kids, or the local dogs, didn't run the bejezus out of them.

An interesting fact is that a hog, if given all the proper

minerals and feed, will balance their own diet. (I think the human species is way behind on that score.) But strangely enough, balancing their diet was why we had a pirate's cave and the origin of this story.

There was some mineral, deep in the soil that our pigs needed to balance their full-meal deal. And believe me, a hog loves to have a bulging stomach. Gary and I noticed the beginnings of a cave about two years earlier where the hogs went down to the creek for water. Whatever the mineral was, apparently that was the only spot with sufficient abundance.

The cave had six feet of soil above the entrance, and the bottom was two feet above the water level during the summer. It was naturally moist and cool in that cave and the hogs tended to eat their clay dirt mineral fill in the mornings. When they'd leave, us kids would head into their special hidey-hole. Well, most of the time we could. But when it was August-hot, the hogs really liked lying in that cool cave for their snooze. Gary and I kept a stout stick or two handy in case they wanted to argue with us.

I know of only one or two occasions where a young hog fought with a human. If there was fighting, it was usually just the mama sows protecting their babies, or maybe a papa boar when deliberately provoked. That was when you'd get a firsthand viewing of their four-inch tusks. And sharp they were, too!

One time the fat hogs did start after us kids and it was scary. I think our dog, Ginger, must have stirred them up. Well, they got to circling us, coming in closer and closer, then making a sound unlike anything I'd ever heard before. My sister, Carol, and cousin, Gary, were there with me and we climbed the fence posts as the dog ran off. More and more of the hogs joined in—on both sides of the fence—woofing and drooling with their big mouths wide open. We were scared! But finally they let up and Ginger, the lucky dog, escaped too.

The next time you see a pig up close—in person or on TV—look at their mouth. It is designed to eat. They can handle an enormous apple as easily as we could eat a cherry.

Jumping ahead a couple of years, this unusual cave was by then ten or twelve feet deep and five feet high, just right for two young pirates and our four-legged hog partners. We thought about digging a little higher than where the pigs could reach, but in wintertime, with the strong currents and rising water, we figured that might cause massive erosion problems. Also, a medium-sized fir was close by and if the hogs kept digging in the same direction, that tree's weight might collapse our fine Carpenter Creek fort.

So, we decided to use the location only when it was too hot for fun in the tree house, and found it to be a good place from which to launch small boats. I had an assortment of homemade boats, not quite a Ritchey Armada, but close and one kinda odd homemade job that, rather amazingly, I still have in my shop. That little boat is patterned after a World War II aircraft carrier that I chiseled out of two by sixes. It is two boards deep, with a wider upper deck made from one-inch material. Two tiny sets of brass hinges allow access to the large, chiseled out hold. I put tar on the joints (one of my uncles referred to that black, sticky stuff as bear shit). The carrier's length was nearly twenty-four inches and about eight inches wide.

The two most striking things about that boat are how unbelievably crude it appears, and that it still floats. I was ten years old when I made it, so I claim youth as my "crudeness" excuse. I loved to chisel things and I still salivate just a little, thinking about grabbing a good, sharp Stanley chisel. I still have the set I purchased nearly forty years ago. These chisels are made of superior steel, with a durable striking end. They were from the top end of the Stanley tool line.

Another type of watercraft Gary and I made were small, light, cedar-shingle boats. We'd point the thick butt-end of the shingle for the prow, and then cut a wide notch out of the thin end. Next we'd put a paddle in the notch using a rubber band that we'd wind up and just let rip. If we had time, we'd stick a mast and flag in the middle. Just imagine the good times we had! Sometimes in the right water currents, we'd launch and then trail our boats downstream, then haul them out by the family garden that was at least two hundred yards away. And if the neighborhood kids came over, we'd have boat races. But most of the time it was just the two of us, and a dog or two.

I'd guess that I made well over half of my early toys, with the help of our neighbor Jonesee, who would help me cut out the forms. I am positive that this pondering and designing process helped me to become a more creative creature.

One other boat I made was cut from a 4 x 4 clear cedar, but it didn't work very well because its bottom was too round. I've known a few people like that through the years; most of them were of the feminine gender.

Gary and I hardly ever swam in Carpenter Creek because by the time the water was warm enough, the water level was too low. We made up for that lack of depth by heading over to Gales Creek, which bordered our farm on the north. Besides, there were more neighborhood girls who gathered along good old Gales Creek. I have a story or two about the goings on taking place on that "body" of water that I'll share with you later.

No Mercy!

"You need to wear suspenders," I shouted derisively to him as his jeans dropped off his bony hips and fell all the way down to the ground.

I guessed, and fervently hoped my luck was changing for the better now. He could not run. But, more importantly, he could not chase me! Maybe I could outrun him, because I was pretty fast for a fourteen-year-old kid.

I had been his hostage for eighteen—*lifetime*—hours, for sure long enough to know I hated him. Every visceral part of him! He had made me listen to the entire litany of his traumatic childhood events that he claimed contributed to what he was... *a frigging queer.* I even hated his incestuous, dominating mother, and his pathetic, weak, alcoholic father. This pervert had owned me!

Their twisted family had moved next to ours a few months prior and my folks—with my younger twin sisters—were spending a long weekend at the coast. My paper delivery job prevented me from going along.

There was only one place for him now—*as he made his beastly trip to hell*—and I would do everything in my power to help him achieve that goal.

We were outside the small storage building where I'd been held captive on rural property owned by his monster family. I was outside now because I had to go to the bathroom. Actually, I'd already gone in my shorts and was looking for any chance to escape.

He still had the knife, but now I had a long stout stick and for the first time since I'd known him, I liked my odds. I think he realized it too by the look on his face. But he was a sly one—maybe his defeated expression was just a ruse. Well, me and the stick and the knife, and his fallen trousers would find out.

Who would make the first move? I was pretty sure he could not throw the knife with any accuracy because I'd seen the awkwardness of his movements. But I would risk a bad cut for a chance to escape and he recognized my desperation!

I made a jab toward his genitals with my stick and he tried to protect them by doing an ungainly awkward hop to avoid the thrust. I poked again. More aggressively! He slashed with the knife, lost his balance, and nearly fell over. I sneered a half-smile to convey my long-sought superiority and he shook his left foot trying to get rid of his stained, dirty old Levis.

I grabbed the stick like a baseball bat and swung with everything I had at knee height. There was a meaty crack, which brought forth a cry of anguish and pain. The sharp impact almost made me drop my weapon. He limped and hopped. The trousers dropped off one foot, allowing him to move more freely.

He flashed a look indicating that he had regained control as he hobbled towards me with the knife. I fenced towards his face, and then backed up rapidly on the uneven ground.

He moved faster, trying to corner me against the old shed where I'd been held captive. Then he stepped on the empty pant leg and tripped, sprawling face forward into the slimy mud. I raised the heavy club end of the limb over my head and brought it down on the back of his neck.

The blow seemed to hurt him severely and he appeared unable to move his lower body.

Not taking a chance, I hit him real hard above the ear with my stick. He made a kind of mewing sound. Then he dropped that damn knife—oh so slowly.

Earlier, he'd held that knife to my face, making a trickle of blood run down my cheek while I was tied to a chair. He had even talked about notching my ear! Then he laughed sickly with his demented hyena-like cackle.

I approached him with caution, grabbed the knife, and threw it into some nearby, dense briars. But, I must admit that I had a brief argument with myself about carving on him a little bit.

I ran to the shed, grabbed some twine, and trussed him

up extra tight. All the while, he was giving me that evil eye of his. I wondered how long it would take in prison for that evil eye to become the begging eye. Like mine had been.

Reflections

In a full length mirror
Or pristine pond
How many times
Have you seen yourself
Coming 'round

Or in your children
As they emulate you
That little gesture
Knowingly or unaware

In the eyes
Of a loved one
Or that special friend
Eyes mirroring
The brightly shining
Window to the soul

With flecks of light dancing
From the joy
Of being together
Inwardly as you smile
At yourself over past conversations
And happy recollections

Watching a puppy
Facing a mirror
Hearing his excited bark
About another pal to play with

A windblown prism
As it captures the diamonds
From the late afternoon sun
Moonlight shimmering on a lake

A lighted path
Leading straight to you
The center of the universe
The never-ending ocean sunset
Casting pink and orange hues

The tips of the waves
Glistening ever so briefly
In the arc of a rainbow
With all of its radiant glory
As God's reflections

The Double Reach

I got help from an unexpected quarter, totally out of the blue—or in this case—out of the black. This unusual happening took place in a college vocabulary class. And before you take that toad-like mental leap, vocabulary was not a basket-weaving course. It had plenty of substance plus genuine old-fashioned learning, as in *memorization*.

The biggest challenge for me was mastering the rudiments—the roots—of words. This requires ferreting out the beginnings and endings in our melting pot of Yankee language stew. Many words are based on Greek or Latin origins, which to me adds both depth and mystical quality. I view it as a connection backwards, like an archeological word dig.

I was striving my very best in this sophomore elective because, one, the class was scintillating—studying the prefixes and suffixes of words. And two, my G.P.A. needed a boost upward. My freshman year was one of scholastic adjustment—mainly adjustment to studying, which I had not done in high school. (Let me clue you in about non-studiers—they do not last long in a major university. There were teachers trying to flunk me out. It wasn't personal, just the law of the higher-learning jungle.)

A vivid memory from my 1958 frosh orientation class goes like this... We were instructed to take a look around at the four people sitting in the chairs immediately surrounding us. The big kahuna orienteer said, "Those four people surrounding you will not be here in four years." And truly, the fun seekers dropped out rapidly, like sick, cloned flies, in each succeeding term.

By the time winter term was half over, my studious efforts were being rewarded and I had an A grade going. This feeling was exhilarating and I wanted to maintain that high-octane charge.

But the jackal pack's attack had started a couple of classes earlier. One guy in particular was jabbing me mentally, and he had a couple of other parasitic kids joining him, nibbling at the edges. I never got a clear picture of their agenda other than perhaps jealousy and, of course, the pack mentality kicking in. None of them had an A on their scholastic horizons, and they'd be lucky to grab a C.

It's hard to describe their hurtful attacks. And it was unusual for me not to not take the bait and respond. I was not known to be a mental or physical pussycat, and in fact, it was unusual for anybody to mess with me. I think all of us, especially in youth, project a demeanor. Our front either invites the jackals or repels advances. My "front" had me in the middle of the road or neutral zone. And for sure, part of the time my hands-off signal was hoisted. But for whatever reason, I did not feel like responding to the leader of that baffling mini-pack.

We always sat in the same seats and in that particular class, a black girl sat behind me. I'd had limited exposure to black people up to that time. Only one black family lived in Forest Grove while I was growing up, and that family left after just a few years. Even during the time I served in the military there were very limited numbers of black trainees.

This was the third time this dorky guy had jumped on my case and I could tell a bad habit had formed. I don't think I'd ever spoken to the black girl, but hopefully I had at least smiled a good morning greeting.

But *SURPRISE!* The black girl confronted all three of those jackals just before class started.

"If you studied as hard as he does, all of your problems might be solved," she told them. There was more, too, which I do not recall. She just dived into the mental fray, focusing on the main aggressor. It was like she was my big sister, protecting me, but she certainly wasn't physically bigger.

She managed to turn that jackal's ears all the way down, and the threesome were stricken to silence not just for that day, but the rest of the term. I did not know what axe that girl was grinding—you'd think she'd have had plenty of her own without borrowing mine. Did I ever understand why she reached out to help me? No. Would I have liked to know? Yes.

A week or so later, I asked her to join me for a Coke at the Commons. I was striving to somehow repay her for her very thoughtful intervention. Strangely, neither of us knew what to say. I don't think she was envisioning bringing me home to dinner, nor was I planning on taking her home to my house. Our brief Coke date started and ended rather awkwardly. Both of us went back to our own little worlds that sadly we break out of only occasionally, and usually that's just to help a close friend. Yet that girl reached out with both hands—a double reach. She offered one hand as a fellow human being and the other hand across the deep ravine of racial divide. My guess is that she had done it before, and she's probably done it many times since.

My perception was that she was that all too rare commodity in the competition of youth—a genuinely nice person. A person who would go out of her way to defend someone being unfairly attacked, as if she had taken a walk in my shoes. The only way I can return her favor, her act of kindness, is to be willing to step in and offer help to other folks.

The "Sparking" Spot, AKA McKibben Lane

Sal and I had made the scene on that sometimes-remote rural spot countless times, mostly on Friday or Saturday evenings 'cause we lived just down the gravel road. Weekends were when this hot spot most definitely couldn't have been considered remote!

The "action" did not occur year-round. Sometimes the weather got too cold or wet for even us farm kids, and the crazy fun I refer to took place outside.

There was just a lot more *stuff* happening on days when runny sweat dripped off the end of your nose during those long, hot summers. Sometimes several cars would park at the spot, then start "sparking," and Sal and I would draw straws on the one or two lucky moonstruck couples to harass.

I, or more accurately, neither of us, liked it when a well-used condom came flying out the back window and barely missed our faces, but we knew that pretty soon it would be our turn. Well kind of. Sometimes it was a two-condom night. Once there were even three. So we had to get used to ducking.

On one particularly steamy evening, an older-model car sure was rocking, even with its crummy old 1940s leaf springs. We had seen this car before but didn't know the male occupant. The erroneously called weaker sex inside seemed to change regularly 'cause sometimes we got a peek when the dome light came on while they were getting re-robed. In my younger days, I used to speculate on how often underpants were put on backwards and inside out.

One of the cutest cars was a 1938 Ford with a Rumble Seat. This hotrod came out only on the warmest of evenings because they used that open rumble seat. Most of the time, somebody's feet would be hanging out the side. There were plenty of times I sure was tempted to reef on a big toe, but always managed to fight off that Irish urge. The car was as hot as its jock owner from Pacific University. We figured he dated only full-figured cheerleaders, and of course, we silently cheered them on.

The name of this popular place was McKibben's Lane. Dense, brushy woods were on both sides of the gravel road, which gave us good cover for our covert activities. There were a few other "sparking" spots in the Forest Grove area such as Higby Lane and David Hill—if you wanted a view, and of course, the old reliable cemetery, but that tombstonie place would not have been high on my list. Besides, Grandma in her grave might have been watching and then coming 'round to have a little chat with me.

Grandma was surprisingly good with those chats. She was also good at "reckoning." I think reckoning is something they did a lot of in Pleasant Grove, Iowa, which is where she hailed from.

Now, I'm sure some of those young couples got tired of our playing around, but they never stopped coming. Their repeated return was a wonderful testimony to human nature and hormones. And Mr. B. F. Goodrich sure was raking in the bucks!

Let me tell you about the most fun night Sal and I ever had out there. Sal was on the slender side, with short hair and as fun loving as me, maybe more so. And she was the one who came up with the trick plan for that night. I think part of our strong bond was our common Irish heritage, and I figure that way, way back we were kinda related. We had been neighbors since we could walk, never anything serious between us, just rousing good friends with a matching sense of country-spun humor.

It was about eight at night and just getting dark in early fall. The bullfrogs were doing their courting too, and going harrumph in the nearby swamp. Fiddle-legged crickets were sawing out their mating song and naturally, pretty soon the windows of the cars fogged over like they someone had pulled down the shades.

Sal and I had been thinking about this brand-spanking new trick for days. We sure hoped we could pull it off without a hitch. So I waited a little while to let the couple in the car get properly engaged—so to speak. Then I crawled under the car pulling a light chain with a gunnysack at the end. I tied the sack-covered end of the chain to the car axle and Sal hooked the other end about five feet up the trunk of a small Fir tree. Then I opened a can of super-smelly Limburger cheese and with heavy leather gloves, liberally smeared gobs of cheese on the slightly warm exhaust system.

The evenings were just starting to get a little white frost on the pumpkins, and we figured it would probably dip close to freezing that night, which would mean starting the car would be a necessity in order to keep the inside toasty warm. And that would, of course, incite those delicious cheese odors, so sooner or later they would leave, or try to. Sal and I, of course, didn't know if the spindly tree would break or just bend and perhaps jerk them back like a big rubber band. Either way it would produce some McKibben Lane laughs for us! And boy, I could easy visualize them dragging that tree down the road, along with some old-fashioned swearing!

In the meantime, Sal and I went to check out another love-happy sparking couple for just another fun-filled evening on McKibben Lane. Especially if we didn't get caught.

The Psych Class

Volumes of sweat poured from every sweat gland and the salt was stinging my eyes. My pulse was racing as I glanced furtively at my classmate who was grading my paper. Frantically, I strove to interpret his reaction. Our class had just completed an intensive psychological questionnaire that included rather personal queries. The questions were ingeniously designed to eliminate faking responses.

The room was full—testimony to the prowess and credentials of the instructor. He was probably in his mid-fifties and one of the most curious, prying individuals I've ever met. In addition to his teaching, he was actively pursuing sexual research and publishing his findings. And he was always trying to get me to reveal my adolescent sexual history. I'd had to make up lies to entertain him, or else tell him about guys I knew. Personally, I thought he was excessively preoccupied and a bit hung up on sexual issues. But at least the instructor and his professional endeavors seemed well matched.

The cause of my profuse sweating can be rolled into one single word—femininity.

The random survey questions were divided into several categories, all to be answered with your first gut response. It took about forty minutes to complete the entire gamut of questions. Then we exchanged our papers with a nearby classmate.

I could see my tally in each column and I appeared to be in the normal range in every one, except... the newly exposed Greek tendon—femininity. I was off the chart in this area!

There had already been substantiated proof I had strong feminine tendencies. A good friend and I had once doubled-dated and attended a sad movie. My friend and I both started blubbering at some emotional scene, while the two girls shed nary a tear. To make matters worse, my own mom used to call me Suzie Q. Now why would anyone do that? And especially a flesh and blood mother? Unless....

My mind spun into warp speed. Did this over-the-top score mean I was a queer?

Note: In the 1950s and early 1960s, the slang word for homosexual was "queer," not "gay." In fact, you could still call someone a "gay blade," and it was a compliment. I'm still bothered that we've lost use of this super neat word.

The paper I was grading did not spike in that column, and I could see the paper of another classmate, a girl, and even she was not in orbit on this girlish subject. So what was the matter with me? I think I knew.

What would I tell my family? My friends? Would I have to come out of this dark, suffocating closet?

Finally, the teacher, Dr. Freud Kinsey, began explaining the categories. It took him forever to get to the column on femininity, and I was bracing myself for more bad news. Rivulets of perspiration still ran down my face. For some perverse reason, he did not address the gender issues in order and saved femininity for last. Then with a smirky smile he said, "Femininity is a measurement or indicator of your sensitivity to people or situations."

Oh, God! What a *relief*, but it was too late. I needed a shower in the worst way. Probably all the estrogen in my system had evaporated, or maybe it was the other way around and all the testosterone had made a detour.

The Stare

The car fishtailed violently from excessive speed. Then it turned completely around, going full speed backwards and careened off the end of the bridge into the deep waters of the flooded channel!

I was on my way home from a night of having a beer or two. Oh, you're right, it could have been three suds, and probably was. My girlfriend and I had been playing pool with another young couple for two bits a game at a local pub. The night was clear and cold and the two long bridges I had to cross to get home were coated with black ice. Western Oregon had been doing its late fall thing—record rainfall the previous week.

I had safely negotiated the first bridge over Crazy Woman Creek and my car's headlights flickered over the hard and brilliant white hoarfrost coating the second bridge. That's when I heard the '53 Ford coming fast, really laying on it. It's flathead V-8 engine was screaming with the prized Fenton headers rolling out their special thunder! I recognized the stylish fleet-back Ford and its driver— Frankie. The car went around me in between the first and second bridges. The insane speed and hoar ice on the second bridge did him in—in more ways than one.

I watched in disbelief as the '53 Ford shot off the road backwards....

Off the road backwards immediately brought to mind a recent incident at the local "watering hole." An older high school classmate had been joshing Frankie about what he enjoyed the most about being a queer. On the surface, Frankie did not take offense, but then he was half-looped and never known to be aggressive. Plus, the older classmate had an unusual knack of being able to say anything to anybody and the "lucky" recipient kept right on smiling, always in a benign manner.

The Ford splashed into the cold, inky black floodwaters. Then it slowly settled at a thirty-degree cant. The angling headlights focused on the North Star. Chilly enveloping waters shut down the beautiful sound of that Ford V-8 engine.

The surreal scene in front of me was a driving display that could have been staged for the "big" screen with Steve McQueen or Clint Eastwood behind the wheel.

I had placed myself in an extremely vulnerable spot in part because I was old enough to drink legally, but it was past tavern closing time and I was guilty of closing those establishments way too many times. Although, being 21 and a college graduate don't necessarily add up to having good sense.

Carefully I pulled over to the wrong lane and rolled down the window alongside the deep ditch. The brisk east wind chilled my face as I peered down at the partially submerged car. There was movement in the front seat. *Good*, I thought. *I won't have to get wet hauling his dumb ass out of there.*

Frankie finally got the driver's side door open and labored his had-to-be bruised body from the soggy wreck. I shouted, "Frankie, why don't you shut the lights off?"

Foggily, he obeyed. Then he snail-slogged his way up the steep bank nearly tipping backwards in the slime and tall grass. My headlights illuminated his wild, red-veined eyes.

Meanwhile, I was casting around frantically for a plan. I *did not* want him in my car—but maybe he had an injury. Finally, and reluctantly, I concluded that I *had* to let him in. Frankie looked like a red-eyed, drowned rat with his scrawny beard and greasy ponytail. He also looked sad and forlorn—it had been a bad night for Frankie.

Frankie was a year older than me, and he'd been an assistant coach for wrestling during high school. I don't think very many kids knew about Frankie's inclinations in high school. I didn't!

This dicey car accident occurred several years after high school graduation and by then Frankie's natural bent was common knowledge in our always-gossipy town.

Everyone knew Frankie was queer, or "gay," as is the correct term today. Gay was not a denigrating word in those long ago days, but "queer" darn sure was! I resent taking the word "gay" away from us straights.

And I want to make my thoughts here very clear. First, I do not wish to offend anyone, but I desire to be historically correct regarding the way it was in our local area, which was probably a genuine backwater. "Queer" was the descriptive word for homosexuals during the mid-1950s. The word "lesbian" had not surfaced yet in our community, and no one I knew had yet conceived that a woman could have similar thoughts or desires.

So, Frankie drenched my car seat where my girlfriend had sat just ten minutes ago.

Frankie was quite obviously drunker than forty dollars. He was like forty dollars times two. His head even wobbled like a bobble-head dashboard doll. The odor of stale cigarettes and booze permeated my car, overpowering my benign pool-playing night out.

I turned my '58 Chevy muscle car around and headed back into town. For some reason I turned on the dome light and watched his left elbow drip onto my seat. Beads of swamp water glistened on his head and hair.

Then *IT* happened! The STARE! The most penetrating, haunting, hell-awful stare I have ever, ever experienced.

I almost drove off the road from that terrible stare.

And then I froze under his heated stare! My mind literally quit working for several eternity-long seconds. All of the little I'd learned about queers flashed through my mind. I felt like I was a tiny mouse and he was a huge predatory lion with his paw raised and mouth open. My body and mind first registered—then suffered—several weird, conflicting sensations but *completely* overriding all of them was his drunken, lustful, terrifying stare.

Finally, and desperately, I pulled my locked eyes away from his penetrating stare. I felt as though I had looked into his aching soul. Then he looked down—and the tense situation defused. My pounding heart slowly stopped racing. I was drained, totally exhausted!

I laboriously negotiated two right turns and a left, then pulled up to the front of the police station and dropped him off. When the car door slammed shut, I breathed the biggest sigh of my young life.

Frankie soon moved away to a larger town—then went to prison for I don't know what. I heard he died a few years later. His small family lived a very low profile life.

I *have* learned how difficult it was to be a queer, especially in those days. And I've learned to feel very sorry for Frankie!

The Probing

It is impossible to know
How many times
Our shovels
Sliced into the clay soil
Each full spade
A small step
Cutting in deeper and deeper
Clods rolling back down

Occasionally we probed
With a bright steel rod
And we knew there was
More distance to go
Then it would happen
Deep in the ground
The shovels would hit an object
Then unearth… a box

A large, oblong box
Weathered, deteriorating
Wormholes throughout
Frantic, we increased our pace
I don't know why

The thing could only be a coffin
Then a creaking
Moaning sound
Oh, no…
The end was falling off….

A Back-Up Plan

The car had been following me down the dark, winding, country road. A slow, drifting fog accentuated the loneliness of the remote area.

I was fast-jogging because my 1989 Pontiac had been acting up again and I had to leave it sitting by the side of the road. It always picked the worst times to conk out. I'd been heading over to spend a night or two with an old girlfriend. That lady and I went way back. Her door almost always swung open for me. My jogging turned into flat-out running when the car following me sped up.

The ghost-like fog made the road seem unfamiliar, but then I recognized the log cabin occupied by an unfriendly, ancient hermit and his guard dog. Just beyond his place, I knew of a back trail along the river to my part-time girlfriend's house. That trail originated on an old pioneer logging road that cut through sparse fir tree cover toward the fast moving Kluchi River. My heart leapt at the thought of an easy escape.

I knew why they were following me—I'd cashed a big check (big for me) at Ray Giltners' neighborhood grocery store at the edge of town. Those two seedy-looking guys had been behind me in the checkout line. One had been lugging a short case of beer. They were either brothers or cousins, because both had narrow slits for eyes and the same receding chin that their scant whiskers couldn't cover. Their piece-of-crap car—when they pulled out to follow me—was even more beat up than my tired Pontiac.

I tried to run even faster, but was already gasping and sucking for air. Too many Camel cigarettes, I guessed. The car pulled onto the old logging road with its headlights shining through the trees. Then I heard them on foot— crashing through the branches and brush—gaining on me. Glancing back, I nearly tripped over a protruding root. Wheezing and groaning, I came up against a deer fence with barbwire on top. *Shit!* I thought. *This damn fence hadn't been here before, when I stopped by a couple of months ago to fish the Kluchi.*

I struggled up the fence and caught my shirt, and then my pants snagged on the barbs. Some of those sharp barbs poked all the way through my worn Levi's. I felt the razor-like steel points penetrate the skin of my upper leg! *"Oh, damn,"* I said to myself.

But, with a little bit of luck, I had one more trick up my sleeve (you always need to have a backup plan.)

That's when I heard my "trick" back-up plan coming, growling low in his huge throat, and he was on the heels of the two guys. Oh, that menacing growl was a *good sound!*

The dog was half wolf, half Great Dane, and the hermit had named him Lobo, which was a good fit. His nose and night vision were vastly superior to his prey.

Lobo caught the slower of the two guys chasing me. I heard a piercing scream, then vicious snarling and snapping! I knew all too well what was happening because I'd nearly been the snack of that intimidating wolf-dog a few months prior.

My trousers ripped and I dropped to the other side of the fence, just as the remaining assailant reached the wire and started to climb up after me. He was panting— laboring harder than me—and his beery breath almost overpowered my senses.

Then I heard that good deep, guttural growl again— accompanied by several low whines—probably sounds of canine anticipation. Lobo was close.

I watched as the dog caught this dorky cull as he frantically scrambled up the fence. Lobo clamped onto the calf of his leg. There was more frenzied screaming and kicking!

I picked up a long stick and rammed it as hard as I could through the fence into the guy's crotch, which was by then at my chest level. I could see the whites of his eyes. They weren't slits anymore! His scream went into a higher pitch. Then his mouth hinged wider, but strangely, no sound came out.

I reversed the stick, which had a big knot at the other end, and smacked him alongside his sorry-looking noggin. I figured their "nippy" problems weren't my concern as I hurried down the trail.

Oh yeah, my old-time girlfriend wanted the whole bloody story when I finally made it to her place, ripped clothes and all, minus my Pontiac.

And the two culls? Well, I really never knew for sure, but Lobo looked like he'd put on a few pounds when I drove by his house a couple of days later. Their beater car was still sitting in the brush.

The Erotic Manure Pile

What follows is a roll-by-roll replay of one of the most bizarre sights I have ever encountered. The risqué rolling I'm about to describe took place almost thirty years ago and it is only now that I've finally gathered the courage to relate the entire (well, most of this) hilarious happening.

I can quite accurately say this barnyard happening was one of a kind and the starring human participant is undoubtedly the happiest now that it is all behind him. Although the heifer cow critter involved probably ran a close second on that "behind" happy scale. It's just too bad that cell phone cameras were not available back then. I would even have paid extra for one that could replicate the cacophony of sounds and pungent, racy odors.

My two longtime partners, Dale Zumwalt and Ron Wade, and I had purchased 110 acres of mostly timberland on Pumpkin Ridge Road in the north part of Washington County. The prior owners, two brothers, had inherited the foothills property from their father. The father had been a knowledgeable farm operator, but the two sons were most definitely not. In fact, on a scale of one to ten, they were hanging on the bad side of zero. The two brothers had retained 120 acres of brushy pasture, including a run-down, two-story farmhouse where the life-long bachelor brother maintained his bare existence. Their property abutted ours. Our property was the westerly portion.

The bachelor brother amazingly had a B.S. degree in agriculture, but his personality was deeply imbedded with a broad streak of laziness that went clear to the bone. He just plain talked everything to death, waxing on eloquently about any farm problem, looking at every conceivable angle, and maybe all of his limited energy was spent just gassing. It could be that the book learning and "BS" degree had led him astray, where I suspect he was easily led, except when it came down to a matrimonial path.

The married brother reportedly had a steady job and lived in the nearby town. And he did drive a well-maintained pickup truck, a rarity for Pumpkin Ridgers in those days. This townie brother even had a pretty nice looking house, but that well-tended look could have been his wife's doing.

Ridge Road residents had a longstanding—and well-deserved—reputation for whelping most of the local outlaws. Everybody living along that road seemed to be related, and I think the gene pool was stagnant because new, quality infusions had been severely limited for a very long time. Ridge Road was definitely not a place one wanted to be late at night, particularly after the taverns closed. The long, snaky road seemed to come directly out of the bootleg whiskey movie *Thunder Road,* which in case you don't remember, starred Robert Mitchum. The yellow road signs were magnets for target practice and resembled low quality Swiss cheese. Likewise, most of the mailboxes were so full of bullet holes they could have served as a sieve. The weekend fights at the Pumpkin Ridge Grange and Dance Hall were legendary. This foothills backwater was obviously struggling, and slowly staggering, into the 20th century.

It was a rain and sunshine mixed December day when I drove out there because I needed to talk with the brothers about a shared fence problem. I saw the town brother near the ancient barn and corral that—in a dilapidated sense— sheltered their beef herd. I need to state here that the barn was in way better shape than the farmhouse. My partners and I had performed our part of the fence project and the brothers were still doing the thing they were best at, jawing. We knew by then that the townie brother had more on the stick, and if you talked with the bachelor brother, you could guarantee that nothing would happen.

The town brother had sired a half-baked kid who was then about eighteen years old, but behaved as if he were many years younger. As I drove up, the kid was playing cowboy with a rope inside the corral. I walked up to the corral fence, which the town brother was leaning on. I could tell he'd had a lot of experience leaning on whatever was handy (there is a certain look), and I figured that maybe he worked for the county road crew.

I assumed my position, with one foot on the lower corral rung, because I've had a little leaning practice, too. Quality leaning isn't something that comes natural to everybody. You need to start young and rub shoulders with the right folks and remember that leaning and spitting go hand-in-hand.

But learning to spit is an art all to itself—just watch any sporting event. I understand that's how the Heisman football trophy winner is really picked. I'm sorry, folks, that I don't have the time to fully address the pure enjoyment and satisfaction regarding properly punctuating your comments with accurate spitting. But know that the spitting does have to be accurate to really get your point across, and the absolute worst thing that can occur is to dribble spit on your chin, especially on national TV.

I had practiced my spitting as I learned to chew tobacco and dip snuff. Chewing tobacco generates a big gob of spit so you'd better be outside. But snuff is stronger—a good pinch under your lower lip is equal to a couple or three beers, drunk fast, but this effect does wear off after awhile. So spitting is part of this deal, too.

Anyhow, the cattle were all riled and stirred up and bawling loudly with steam rising from their curly winter coats. The odor of manure came on like an avalanche, assaulting all my senses with a savage intensity. Fleeting rays of sunlight flashing diagonally into the corral accented this steaminess.

I looked around for the cause of the cattle commotion and bellering.

The brothers had the misfortune to own, (or maybe it was the cows' misfortune to be owned by the brothers) seventy-five head of pitiful looking whiteface cows. At first glance, they appeared to suffer from Arkansas in-breeding and a lack of feed. I knew darn well that part of the problem was that their crummy pasture was choked with tansy ragwort weed. Cows will not eat this noxious weed unless starving, but if consumed, it affects their liver. The liver damage can result in severe stunting or death, depending upon the amount eaten. As proof, my partners and I had found several animal carcasses littering our newly purchased timberland. The brothers also had twice too many cattle pasturing on the very sparse grass, and the only fertilizer applied was recycled cow crap.

It gets worse.

For some unfathomable reason, the brothers had not castrated their bulls. One cannot sell an uncastrated bull because the meat has a strong unpleasant taste. This lazy oversight, or under-do, resulted in buku of bulls, all sizes and ages. The tansy ragwort had stunted the bulls, some of them dramatically. Some were several years old, but the size of a small Shetland pony. They ranged in stature from miniature, to nearly full size, and if sufficient feed had been available, maybe a few would have been full size.

Right after I'd gotten comfortable with my version of the proper leaning position, a neighborhood kid came over on his Honda. He was a little older—or at least bigger—than the mutton-headed cowboy kid. There was something quite unusual about this neighbor boy—his lips. He had a gigantic pair of lips. I think the lips were a direct result of the limited gene pool, judging by his folks, but I can't rule out lip-enlargement surgery. I could not look at the kid without grinning, and he'd always grin back. He was good-natured and laughed a lot.

I then saw what was causing the animal ruckus—a runty heifer was in heat. Cows are like women, with the same 30-day intervals and nine-month pregnancies.

The mutton-headed kid was still playing cowboy with that heifer, and his townie dad was encouraging his dismal efforts of trying to rope the young heifer and separate her from the other weird looking bovine critters. There were twenty-five stunted bulls milling around and they were getting sexually aroused.

The kid got real unlucky when he caught the heifer—not around the neck, but by tangling her feet. She immediately fell over into a mound of manure. Then, the would-be cowboy got his own feet tangled in the rope and he fell down next to the heifer. Luckily, the rolling was soft and he started groping to get a foothold. By then, the menagerie of bulls were pawing and milling in a sexual frenzy. The bellering bulls and the bawling heifer turned into a full animal orchestra.

I could see the whites of eyes of the kid and the heifer as they both rolled frantically in the manure mound. The bulls kept snorting and bellering, with the little ones darting in and out, and being pushed aside by the bigger bulls. All the bulls were, by then, fully aroused. The tansy ragwort hadn't harmed that part of them, it seems.

The bull activity ramped up several more notches because the stunted heifer was immobilized. The bulls' nostrils flared, their necks were fully distended, and full-throated roars erupted from their mouths. There was so much heat and steam rising that the animal chaos looked like a small volcano.

I had been trying mightily to contain myself and finally I could not control my mirth any longer. I just burst out laughing, completely losing my favorite leaning position. The big-lipped kid joined right in and pretty soon, the townie dad lost it, too. I suppose it's a God's wonder that the wannabe cowboy kid wasn't trampled or kicked.

Pretty soon, the thoroughly dung-bedraggled kid and the shaken heifer got up and started running. All the bulls trailed them, creating total pandemonium. The last I saw of the kid, the heifer, and the bulls were their rear ends as they all disappeared into the cavernous old barn.

That was probably the runty heifer's first experience with sex, and gosh knows what was going through her bovine mind. She'd have quite a story to tell mama cow later on. Cows do talk, ya know.

All I can say is... be careful with what you try to lasso.

Out Of Step

Some things are predestined. I kinda knew from the get-go about the military and me. I was oil; the military was water.

I *hated* being told what to do. I've probably spent more time out of step than synchronized with any military unit—be it squad or platoon or company or battalion. There were times I thought the master sergeant from Georgia would make a recording for me that said, "Get in step, Ritchey!"

I'd long suspected I had clumsy, out-of-step tendencies. My first concrete clue was in high school gym dance class—Fred Astaire I was not. So, after high school, my friend Thomas Tomkins Paterson and I joined the Army Reserve because they had the shortest time commitment anyone could serve and still fulfill their happy draft obligations. The Reserve had a six-month active duty requirement, similar to the National Guard. Anybody can do 180 days, standing on his head, right? Wrong! One hundred and eighty days turns out to be an eternity!

Oh, I skated on most of the Army requirements such as making a military-style bed, spit polishing my shoes, and shining my belt buckle. Their Plan A was to mold me into the very best our fine country has to offer. But that was not to be. I was a true square peg in a round Army foxhole, and a group of low-life cadre delighted in making fun of me. My ruddy complexion drew their malicious attention and I became known as "Hamburger Face." Little did they know they were rousing many generations of Irish genes.

The cadre people were genuine hardheads who had been broken in rank several times, resulting in mean malcontents. Their primary purpose in military life was to make us peons miserable. I would have enjoyed a timely chitchat with their mother about some much needed fetching up, obviously absent during their formative years.

Initially, one has no recourse—you simply absorb and endure the abuse, ignoring the jibes as best you can. In my case, I simply turned another red cheek, but just walking in the chow line was a chore for me and I was clumsier than a cub bear. Maybe my feet were ambidextrous and my left foot wanted to be my right foot. I think I can blame my dad for my foot dexterity. He probably wasn't good military material, either.

So I endured the grueling and endless weeks spent whipping us nincompoops into shape. Well, as close to military shape as I would ever be. (Aside: when you are eighteen, a week is a snail-like month, but now that I'm in my seventies, a month gallops along like a day.)

The Asian flu was making the rounds in 1957. It took a toll on our ranks, with guys falling over as we marched. Some even died. The ones who lived were ever so fortunate—they got to repeat several weeks of basic training. Can you imagine the rotten luck?

One fellow who survived did not like regular showers. In fact, he did not like any kind of water combined with soap. Back then, our bunks were arranged alphabetically and that guy's name started with an "O," so it was several days before I got whiff of him. With the already stale male bunkie odors, he ripened up quick! And that army chow wasn't agreeing with that guy, neither. I felt kinda sorry for my friend Tom, whose bunk was a lot closer.

So, it came to pass that several guys baptized him with GI brushes, which were capable of removing car paint. When they were done with the scrubbing, the fellow was pastel pink. Amazingly, his Norwegian mule-stubborn nature required a second currying due to the fact that he was reluctant to get the cleanliness message the first time.

The military is designed to initiate and maintain obedience, supposedly to create strong buddy-bonding morale. Which means everybody at the low end of the army food chain pulls K.P. duty. And it is a fact that some of the cooks were certifiably crazy, which could have been due to their hemorrhoids. I think all military cooks parade around with gigantic suppositories, or they should. On the other hand, military cooks do a marvelous job with that old breakfast standby, Shit-on-a-Shingle, but no matter what, that supposedly nourishing substance is hard to disguise.

My favorite chore was cleaning the sidewalk with a toothbrush. This waste of person-power (exclusively man-power back then) could have changed the universe. But I think none of my extra TLC efforts helped Fort Ord one bitsy iota. A close second for my favorite chore was policing an area wearing just a helmet on my head, sans the liner. This allows the helmet to set on the bridge of your nose, and causes it to flop and bang against your ears. Your vision is limited to just a few feet on each side. It took some military genius months to devise this jolly maneuver. However, I was still able to accomplish a significant amount of buddy bonding with the blinder-wearing idiots on both sides of me, but was careful not to let the cadre catch me in the act of all that BS-ing.

Then, an unexpected bright spot appeared on the bleak and monotonous Fort Ord horizon. It happened on the firing range, with our M-1 rifles. Trainees are taught to fire from four different positions and three distances—100, 300 and 500 yards.

Half the time is spent coaching your partner, and then you switch about. There are also numerous cadre firing line coaches training each soldier—first about safety, then care and maintenance. Finally, you get to shoot.

The firing line coaches have binoculars to see where your bullet hits. Personnel downrange in the bunkers also have pointers to indicate where your bullet strikes. A black pointer depicts a shot that hit within the target; a red pointer signifies a complete miss. This worst miss was called "Maggie's Drawers." Only a four-star general could tell you where that name came from, probably because he was on a first name basis with this certain Maggie. How else could he recognize those drawers at 500 yards? Undoubtedly, that general wound up being a presidential advisor or the Secretary of Defense.

Every army-issue rifle fires in its own unique particular way, and you have to sight them in. Moving the elevation and windage makes the necessary adjustments. (Note: out on the range, after a "shingle" breakfast, someone was always making wind.) Hopefully, each solider continues to modify those rifle factors as distance changes. Some nerds never did get the hang of this simple chore, but it might have been just a put-on so that the nerdies would get assigned to army supply instead of sent to the front lines.

Well… what do you know! It turned out I could shoot! There were plenty of gnat's asses to testify on that score. The firing line coach thought I was Sergeant York from World War I. But I won't let the pride-conscious military take credit for my marksmanship skills. Those scraggly gnats flying around when I was a youngster were spotted first with my 1949 Red Ryder BB gun, then with my .22 rifle. I was so good, I could toss tin cans in the air and ping them with my BB gun. The ricochet would hit the gnat's rear-end and it's a wonder the earth isn't out of orbit with all the lead I expended as a kid.

This consummate skill turned out to be my butt saver, and at the other end, my Irish red cheeks. I could actually see the unrepentant cadre changing their estimation of me—it was mirrored in their normally hung-over, red-veined eyes. They correctly concluded that this farm-boy private might save their worthless skin in the real thing. Actual combat. Anyhow, the good ole sarge from Georgia, he cut me some slack too. But I sure wasn't going to let them talk me into re-upping, or becoming a career dude. We weren't *that* synchronized.

The Peeing Match

This weird incident is still difficult for me to believe it occurred, mostly because of my friend's personality. However, one might want to consider our "tender" age of nineteen, AND the boredom, AND the 90-plus degree heat, AND that we were in between our Freshman and Sophomore years of college, AND that we were in the Yakima Firing Center fulfilling our military obligation, which somehow sucked even more then, AND the vast quantities of cheap Army beer. Yes, *especially* consider the chug-a-lug cold, clear, golden Tumwater Olympia beer!

My very good friend, Thomas Tomkins Paterson—who I partially introduced you to in the previous story—and I were at summer camp courtesy of the U.S. Army Reserves, stationed in hot "deserty" central Washington in August. Yakima appears to have been fashioned at the rear end of creation and it even smells like it, which we found out when we mistakenly dug those latrines upwind. AND especially for boys "reared" (haven't you always thought this was a strange word? I mean, I've almost been reared a couple of times, but somehow, with my Irish luck managed to escape).

Well, anyways, we were that other kind of "reared" in God's country of Western Oregon.

In those days, every man-jack had to do military time, even those who could barely zip up their pants, but then that's why all military clothes had only buttons because they (the upper brass) (notice I did NOT say "brains") knew the range of caliber for happy recruits from all those previous Alamo's, and we had to meet on two Monday nights plus one full Sunday a month to fully contemplate our good fortune.

I'd guess the I.Q. of the recruits was from about 80 to 180. I don't know what the score was for those who deliberately shot off a finger, or those who snuck out to Canada. Anyhow, after the Monday and Sunday stuff, we had two weeks of undiluted summertime Hell at some destination like Yakima. I've always figured the Army stole this location back from the Indians because it was so darn desolate and worthless like everything us whites "gave" to the natives. The other thing of note is that no meetings would be taking place now on Monday nights because pro football owns it.

Naturally, my friend Tom liked to drink beer every bit as much as me, maybe even a shade more because he'd started earlier in life on his imbibing career. But it was all for a good cause, one reason being that I never could figure out which was more fun—the drinking or the peeing. Now

I know I'm getting a little highbrow for some folks, but when you have ample time, just roll that thought around, or, better yet, have a little fun and experiment for yourself. I'll wager some of you might think the two taken together runs a close second to sex, but I caution you not to try all three at the same time.

Yakima that year was a typical desert—hot, hot, and more hot. Sixteen hours of heat wave every day, with the sagebrush giving off its stinking, pungent creosote odor. Good ole Captain Kuffman would order us to crawl through that sagebrush, just to get his officer jollies.

Tom and I were bored silly, and not so strange— considering all our training—we had managed to out-drink the other dumb reservists, so the outdoor PX became empty except for Tom and me and a long, tall, stringy guy whose name has faded into beer oblivion. And Tom probably won't remember either, but maybe by some freak chance that string-bean guy will read this story and call me up. He might even want to smack Tom a time or two after I tell you what happened, which was totally out of character for good-natured Thomas T. (I never saw him get upset but once, but that's another rather rank (but true) tale with yours truly on the receiving end of Tom's mad-on.)

I suppose it was after eleven at night, with reveille coming at six a.m., but we were young and stupid AND, as Mom used to say, burning the candle at both ends. We had already been to the hand-dug latrine three or four times, and in truth, could barely navigate. We probably sidled along like crabs or walked ape-fashion before apes got the hang of walking upright.

Then all three of us—me, Tom, and String Bean—got to talking about having to go... with me always having a bladder with looser strings then most. Besides, I've told you before that peeing is real high on my list of fun things. I don't remember who started first, probably me, but we all joined right in, kinda like it was a chorus to a good old country song. We just unbuttoned our Army-issue khaki green fatigues and let her rip.

We were all grinning great big ear-to-ear grins from relief as all that warm pee washed onto the rock floor. Then the string-bean guy said, "My pants are getting all wet and warm!" And Tom piped right up, "Well, you know what you're doing, don't you?" And String Bean slowly said, "Yes, I allow that I do." But I wasn't so drunk as to not notice that Tom had a bigger grin than usual on his always ready-to-smile face.

I'll interject here to say that almost all boys of my generation have stood on a log or on a line with other boys to see who could pee the furthest, or spit and hit whatever we were aiming at and, of course, whoever could fart the loudest or longest. Ya, all that extra dumb, down-home stuff.

Anyways, we decided to crawl home and hopefully not

puke in our special Army surplus therapeutic bunks. So Stringy staggered off towards his "bude'wa," and Tom and I kinda hung on to each other in an attempt to reach our grand living quarters, while trying not to wake up the other retarded noncoms. But Tom started giggling as we staggered along and he sez, "I peed all over his leg."

I said, "No, you didn't!"

Now, this peeing act was completely and totally out of character for Tom, so I plied him again, but got the same affirmative—

"I peed all over his leg."

Tom *never* lied. Not even little white fibs that could keep you out of that grand, golden place in the sky, but maybe not allow you to sit right next to God. I must emphasize that my friend Tom is flat-out the most honest person I ever encountered.

That's what really happened out there in that forsaken Yakima desert almost sixty years ago. Although you'll probably have trouble getting T.T. Paterson to fess up.

Brüt Force

Pig odors know no enemies! They befriend all. The smell in my small, shared Oregon State University dormitory room was overpowering! It grabbed hold of your nostrils and hung on like a vise. This incredibly offensive odor permeated the clothes hanging in your closet and saturated your bedding. Nothing was immune! It even layered onto the more durable objects such as chairs, desks, and walls—every exposed surface was smothered and tainted.

I had taken a job in the hog barns at the OSU swine department to augment my severely deprived student income during my sophomore year. As pig factories go, this animal research facility would have rated in the pristine column—if hog housing could ever be pristine. And the barns would have been considered "green" in today's world—there was certainly ample green offal to go around.

Although all of the pens were cleaned at least once a day, I need to say it just plain and simple—pig shit stinks. To say nothing about the indescribably bad odor of a boar hog! I'm reminded of a crude farm saying that describes boars and ram goats—"Their odor can knock a buzzard off a gut wagon." The school had several because the professor in charge, a Dr. England, was trying to develop a new breed. Dr. England was combining the Berkshire breed with a couple of others, but his experiments were destined to fail in part because of a disease factor.

Oregon State University (called Oregon State College back then) was known as the Cow College until 1970, although it did offer a few learning pursuits other than agriculture. And the school's stellar idea was to throw all of us who hoped to become future farm leaders of the world into a smoldering pot in the ancient Waldo Hall dormitory.

My roomy was lucky in his draw of a roommate, and his girlfriends got even luckier. This lad was most definitely not short of lady friends. That is, until we got into the gutter tough, turf battle of our fragrances. My junior class roommate was a pompous, testosterone-filled Don Juan, and I had a pervasive trailing odor of hog.

Don Juan's lady-killer personality was incredibly smooth and debonair. He easily met the requirements of dark and handsome, but he wasn't quite on Hollywood star level. He stood ramrod erect, and the elevated heels made him appear taller. He was so punchy proud of his long, black wavy hair worn slicked back like Gregory Peck's, that his comb never had a rest. In fact, I suspect by now, unless he is bald, he has third degree carpel tunnel syndrome in his right hand. His ebony eyes laughed, danced, flashed, and totally engaged the weaker sex. And his jaw line matched Robert Redford's—every woman's heartthrob at that time. He also had a thin, aquiline, slightly hooked nose that projected a haughty, dominating appearance. I suspect there was probably a Spanish gene or two in the remarkable protrusion centered above his mustache.

Dominique was his surname.

He seemed to be magnetically attractive to genuine blondes—sexy, sleek, sensuous blondes. And they apparently were irresistible to him. Typically, he and all the members of his harem ignored me if we chanced to pass on campus. I never was clear on how he managed to get in any focused studying or test preparation time because they were always heading to the library to "study" together. OSU must have had quite a library! And a room I did not know about.

No question, Dominique, or Slick as I called him, was one silver-tongued stud. He's probably gone into politics. He had an answer for everything and his responses were always framed with sexual connotations. Even farm-boy me—straight out of the sticks of Forest Grove—caught some of his horny innuendoes. Slick was convinced he was put on this earth to make women happy, and that I was a doofus hick.

Well, gradually, Slick's friends stopped coming by our dorm room. That was probably due to my excessive pig-parlor scents. But what could I do? My foul, rank odor was being absorbed from close proximity to two hundred research hogs.

Slick took to zipping his school clothes into heavy plastic bags, which he stored in another room. Meanwhile, in the spirit of cultural cooperation, I began showering twice a day... and eating lots of beans, just to toss in a slightly different aroma.

What I should have done was purchase stock in men's cologne because Slick poured on so much that he smelled as though he lived in a whorehouse. Me, with my layered omnipotent pig smell, was at severe risk of nose organ overload, which is when the men's cologne Brüt was conceived!

That whole wing of Waldo Hall breathed a collective sigh, and some fresh air, when I took early retirement from the OSU hog parlor the following term.

Roscoe And Butch

Roscoe's day did not start well and it just kept going downhill. His fixit-repair business had more than its share of problems with both the local and national economy in a protracted slump. The only reliable employment in the community was at the nearby state prison and he hated the thought of working there. He lived with his mother who still thought of him as a little boy, even though he was on the shady side of thirty.

The only constant highlight for Roscoe was his dog, Butch. He and the dog had become very close and they went everywhere together. Butch had worked for the downstate Cutlass City police until his on-duty injury. The dog was highly trained to act on command. Roscoe loved him, even though Butch would never run at full speed again.

The pair was on their way home to his mother's place in the country late on Friday evening. The repair job had lasted much longer than anticipated and he certainly had more hours into the repair than his bid covered. And he wasn't at all sure about how "bouncy" the check was that he'd tucked into his pocket. There'd been just too many downward glances by the old lady client, and she'd had her nose in the booze before the afternoon soaps were finished.

Then Roscoe remembered he'd better fetch his mother her biweekly lotto ticket at the 7-Eleven. A hard-driving rain was slanting onto to his windshield, and he could hear thunder off in the distance as he pulled into the store's parking lot. Butch whined and settled back down in the back seat to wait. He knew the 7-Eleven ritual.

Roscoe made his usual lotto purchase and grabbed a mustard-filled hotdog while Sara, the clerk, flirted outrageously with him, as she did every Friday. The idea that maybe he should consider the next step flitted by, but his built-in bachelor's resistance quickly overcame the desire to ask her out for a date. She might get the wrong idea, although he guessed the weekly flirting was a fleeting pleasure rather than the end game for her.

As he was leaving, Sara said, "Have you heard about the escaped convict?"

"No," Roscoe replied. He figured the few escapees always ran towards the more remote hills to the north.

The early fall storm had gotten even more intense and was unleashing torrents of rain as he exited the store. Roscoe mused, *Well, I'll just have more roofs to fix.*

Roscoe opened his pickup door and was halfway in when he was slammed violently against the doorpost. Something sharp was pushed into his cheek and a menacing voice rasped in his ear, "Just move real slow and easy or I'll kill you."

Roscoe obeyed.

The nasal voice said, "I'm going to slide into the back seat. You drive where I say and maybe... you can live."

The assailant opened the back door of the pickup and Roscoe screamed, "Butch!" The large dog sprang up in full attack mode....

Harry Jackson's Backhoe

This wooden backhoe was designed and built to scale by Harry Jackson of Lincoln City, Oregon.

Construction of the fully functioning tracks alone took more than five years. Those tracks even sound like old time squeaky cat tracks. And the hydraulic system is a quaint example of beauty and design. Harry has since passed away due to the toxic finishing sprays that lined his lungs. This incredibly neat toy was among numerous works Harry built.

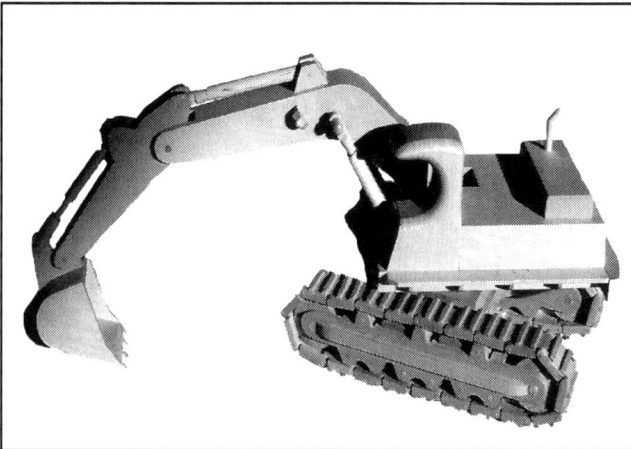

Harry Jackson's backhoe
"Dirt Men" are those who run (or ran) this hoe and other earth-moving equipment

Dirt Men

I've known a few special men
In a class by themselves.
The first was Forest Grove's Dean Haller,
One of the biggest characters
God and the Basque people ever borned
And then put on the seat of a backhoe
Mounted, unbelievably, on a tiny Ford 4N tractor.
Dean could pick your teeth like a hygienist.

Gaston's Gene Hoodenpyle is next.
I learned a lot from him, too
Mostly about constructing logging roads,
Water movement and such,
Like slowing or stopping erosion
Sometimes accomplished with
A fifteen-foot curved fir limb
Eliminating the deep and destructive water bar.

Another chip off that stubborn Oregon block
Was Bank's very own Frank Spiering,
A dirt-moving politician.
We always had to discuss in great detail
Which democratic senator or president
Required the biggest diaper
Finally, after moving to the Devils Lake area
I got well acquainted

With the Haft family from Otis.
Father George and son Justin
Are both throwbacks to another, better time.
George talks so drawly slow
You'd swear rainwater will run uphill.
And Justin is wound and rewound
Tighter than an eight-day Seth Thomas clock.

What do these men
Have in common?
First, they were all straight up.
They each had a marvelous funny bone.
None of them, when the last clod stopped rolling
Will need a re-do.

I thought these men needed more background and so included the following interesting information because each was a character.

Dean Haller was simply one of the quickest and funniest people I've ever known. And when he quit backhoeing in his fifties, he began designing and making wooden signs. He and his daughter, Marie, made the gigantic 10-foot by 14-foot wooden signs still in place as you enter Lincoln City. He's even made several elaborate signs erected way back East. An oddity about Dean—and there were several—is that he paid his bills once a year, whether they needed it or not. He was also the first guy I heard utter the saying, "Friday's payday and shit don't run uphill."

Gene Hoodenpyle spent all his life associated with the logging industry, much of it on "Cats"—D-fours, D-sixes, and D-eights. But he could bring the entire timber crew for falling, cutting to length, hauling, and cleanup—where each procedure is extremely critical to maximizing profits. Gene died much too young from colon cancer, something I believe "cat skinners" are prone to.

Frank Spiering, like all of them, walked pretty slow, but could think darn fast. One thing I enjoyed most about Frank—or Francis, as his sister, Susan, called him,—was the sparkle in his eyes. Those eyes of his jumped out at you and penetrated. You knew you were both 110 percent engaged, when in a discussion with him. He was not too shy, and maybe quick to disagree, but it was always in a "Frank slick" manner. Later, Frank got into the storytelling business and it turned out, he was a natural.

George Haft conveys an immense feeling of loyalty to people and jobs—and boy, could he ever ramrod a job. George started out in logging, too, mostly running the loading rig, which is what sets the rapid pace and definitely affects the dollar outcome of the whole daggone show. The head loader is usually the first person on the job, sometimes at 2:30 in the morning. After being a loader, George got into the "hoe" business. George also works with wood and does some of the prettiest finish work you'll ever see—if you get an invite into their bedroom.

119

George's son, Justin Haft, is a landlord for bottom-end homes and he manages to put up with—and stay ahead of—all the nutty things tenants tend to do, or sometimes don't do. He also is a tree topper for trees in dangerous predicaments, and is spectacular on a hoe. Justin runs everything flat out—so I tend to think his equipment has to be "Haft-Tough."

And all of these guys have—or had—a God-given eye for the precise percentage grade, slopes, and ditches—like who "flung the chunk" (which means really doing or finishing a job—those men were the best of the best). The other commodity they all had aplenty of was something in short supply today—Common Sense.

The Volunteer Payback

I was so happy
When I first saw it
My overriding thought was,
How can this volunteer be here?
Did it fall from the sky?

Probably a bird dropped it
Maybe a Steller's Jay
Or perhaps a raucous crow
But how did the corn seed get buried
In my feeble coastal garden?

Me…who has enjoyed
And labored over many gardens
In a far better clime
Since a wee child
Why even my diapers were soiled
With downtown Dilley dirt

The lone corn plant paired
With my single cherry tomato
Planted next to the house for heat
The doe and fawns love my greens
So no Joseph's Coat Swiss chard

But cherry tomatoes I still enjoy
Strangely, even into December
I picked before the hard frost
Corn that grew to more than 5 feet tall
As I watered, hoed, and fertilized

Eventually three tiny ears formed
And self-pollination occurred
Oh, not very many kernels
But enough that I husked
The cobs and took them to

My Rhode Island Red chickens
Out on rock-strewn Schooner Creek
So the volunteer seed came from a bird
And went back to a bird
Thankfully, I'm easily pleased
And rather punchy proud too!

Just Around the Corner

His bent, frail body was slowly rocking back and forth in his favorite chair near a sun-lit window. The large pane of glass framed their remote farm of nearly 260 acres. His age and state of mind were such that even the chair movements were feeble. The chair's wooden arms were worn smooth by the constant rubbing of his gnarled, arthritic hands. This movement, perhaps an unconscious reflex, seemed to help him ponder… *What will happen to me next?*

The old man's daughter from The Dalles had her own plans for him—the farm would be sold. She'd made that plain when she called me, a rural appraiser.

His cheeks were sunken. Thin, blotchy skin stretched over prominent cheekbones and a few wispy white hairs tried to cover the top of his head. A darkened pipe and ashtray lay on a small side table. I could smell the aroma of Prince Albert Tobacco. (My Grandpa Mac McCue's favorite as he, too, sat in a special chair by a south-facing window.)

The old man's eyes occasionally spoke a resigned glint as they peered at me and my wife. Those sad eyes knew he'd seen better days. He knew he would not be calling the shots anymore.

His old dog lay on the rope rug nearby. Mostly asleep he was, just now and then opening a slow, faded eye to peer at his master. They were a pair, each lonelier now with the missus in her recently mounded grave. A few plants he'd received as gifts after her death occupied the window ledge.

Their home was simple but spotless and homey with the low arcing winter sun shining in the window, striking and briefly warming the old man and dog. Many framed family photos stared down from their places on the dated wallpaper, all those growing up pictures with best clothes, combed hair, and scrubbed faces. An ancient woodstove warded off the late winter chill; his daily supply of dry wood was close by.

He and his wife had raised their three children on the acreage and worked that ground for over forty years. Their only boy, whose handsome military picture was on the wall, had died in Vietnam. I don't know why, but the eyes of young man in the photo caught my eyes, maybe because that war was my generation's horrible military mistake.

The old place and his few words spoke volumes to me. I understood their efforts through the long, hard years because I hailed from a backbreaking farm too. And I knew what that stinky sweat smelled like. I knew about the rocks piled high in the fencerows, almost negating the need for a wire barrier. Each stone had been exposed by farm equipment, or weather, then pried out and carried to the fence line. Every etched stone was a miniature tombstone to their enduring backbreaking efforts. I knew the marks on the stones had been caused by a plowshare or disk. The soil out there was poor, probably just one step above the dirt that holds the earth together. But they had turned hardscrabble into a meager living with daylight to dark toil, frugality, and unrelenting worry.

I knew, without a doubt, that the years required to pay off their farm mortgage had been many, destroying lesser folks.

I respected him.

He was a rarity. An honest man who knew what was… just around the corner.

This story is just a partial picture of how a young rural couple grew old wrestling a living in a tough, tough place in Oregon. I drive by their former farm every so often and still tear up remembering him.

============

The following story is by my wife, Joan. I have always said she has more talent in her little finger than I do in my entire body.

The Old Man
by Joan (Michalke) Ritchey

Still groggy, the man woke from his afternoon nap and surveyed the surroundings of his small studio apartment as he remained in bed. He stretched his arms and then checked his arthritic legs and aching feet. Everything, though still painful, remained the same—no better, no worse. He rolled from his back to his side, moved his legs into a fetal position, then inched his way up into a sitting position on the side of his bed. He reached over and grasped his constant companion, his cane.

Standing beside the bed and leaning heavily on his cane, he put one foot in front of the other and shuffled to the bathroom, the only other room in his house. He looked in the mirror above the sink and, while combing his thinning gray hair, caught sight of the ash-white face with sunken cheeks. He still expected to see a tall man, but now he was shortened by age and permanently arched forward at the waist.

Old Man was what he called himself whenever addressing that face in the mirror.

He moved slowly to the front door of his apartment,

opened it and walked out; counting the twenty-five steps down the hallway that would lead him to the front entryway of the retirement center and to the outdoors. The receptionist was on duty behind the counter in the foyer.

As usual, the old man doffed his crumpled black hat and flashed his crooked smile as he slowly passed the receptionist and made his way out the front door for his afternoon walk.

The old man squinted through half-blind eyes at a young boy riding his bike on the sidewalk. He guessed the boy was half a block away, but with his poor eyesight, the kid could have been much closer.

The boy had been riding his bicycle for twenty minutes. He'd seen the man out walking on other occasions at this time of day.

As the old man limped nearer, the boy dismounted his bike, leaned it up against an oak tree, put down the kickstand for reassurance, and then sat cross-legged on the grass. His bicycle was new, a sleek shiny, apple green. His parents had surprised him with it on his tenth birthday, two weeks prior.

The old man watched the boy as he stood up, took a rag from his back pocket, and began flipping imaginary dust from the fenders and handlebars of his shiny bike. It brought back memories of the bicycle the old man had received as a young boy on a long-ago Christmas morning.

His parents had stood together, arm-in-arm, smiling broadly as their only child mounted his cherry-red bicycle and then took off down their long gravel driveway, riding out onto the paved road adjacent to their farmhouse.

Now, with his ever-so-slow gait, the old man approached the young lad and stopped. He smiled his crooked grin, all the while eyeing the boy's bicycle longingly. He could not believe his ears when the boy asked, "You wanna ride my bike?" He was even more surprised when he heard himself answer, "Uh huh!"

The boy moved his bike to the sidewalk and held it steady while the old man painstakingly lifted his shaky bowed leg over the crossbar. When the old man was seated, the young boy took the cane and held it while the old man shoved off.

He was a youth again! Sitting upright and straight as he pedaled his cherry-red bike down the sidewalk. Before he knew it, he had ridden a half-mile. The wind was cool on his face, his arthritis pain and aching joints went unnoticed. He sat tall and erect as he rode.

The young boy walked very close behind the old man as he pedaled. The bike was wobbling precariously, wheels unsteady and swaying from side to side. The old man was hunched over, knees outward, bowed at the sides of the bike and elbows pointing straight out from the handlebars. The old man looked like a stick figure resembling an "X" from behind. The boy became afraid that the old man would crash and was glad when the ride came to an end after only one block.

Out of breath, but excited, the old man retrieved his cane and began the amble back toward home.

The young boy walked his bike alongside the old man, as reassurance in case the old man would fall.

The old man was young once more, wondering why he even needed his cane.

The young boy was glad the old man had his cane. He needed it for support with every limping, tentative step.

At the front door of the retirement center, the young boy said goodbye as he reached to shake the extended thin, gnarled hand of the old man.

The old man entered the retirement home walking tall and straight, a purpose to his step. He grinned, doffed his crumpled black hat, and winked at the receptionist. She smiled back at the bent man as he painstakingly walked, leaning hard on his half-white cane, down the hallway to his room.

The old man entered Room #105 feeling young, alive, and no longer lonely. The young boy had made him feel happier than he'd felt in weeks. He went to the only other room in his apartment and stared at the reflection in the mirror over the sink. He saw no wrinkles on the plump, pink-flushed cheeks and smiling blue eyes of the face before him. He turned and made his way into his living quarters.

The mirror watched as the old man hobbled to his bed. It was the first time the mirror had ever lied.

The old man opened the window in his room and breathed in the cool autumn air. He turned, took the nine steps to his bed, sat down, and removed his shoes. He laid his head on the plumped up pillows of his newly made bed. The smell of bleach was heavy on his linens, but he quickly replaced it with the sheet and pillowcase aromas from his mother's outdoor clotheslines. He thought how nice it was to come home to a clean room.

The old man closed his eyes and reminisced about his ride today, of his love for his cherry-red bicycle, and other memories of his boyhood years. He returned a grin to the smiling faces of his envisioned parents as they stood arm-in-arm, gazing down lovingly at their only child.

The girl from the receptionist desk arrived at his room to walk the old man down to the dining room for dinner that night. She entered Room #105 smiling and thinking how peaceful the old man looked as he lay there sleeping.

A beautiful wreath hung outside the door of Room #105 the next morning. The inscription on the ribbon-tied card read, "The Old Man Has Gone Home."

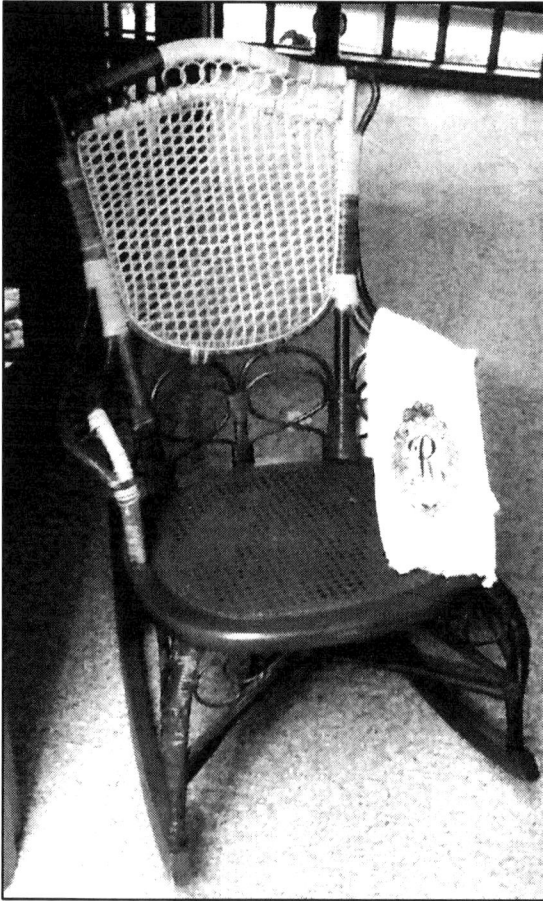
Grandma Ritchey's rocking chair

Stories about Grandma Ritchey were included in my first book, "Hankering For The Way It Was," where I referred to her as a major force in my life. My wife, Joan, wrote the following poem about Grandma Ritchey's wicker rocking chair and now our son, Kevin Cline, has composed a song based on the poem. We are eagerly waiting for the recording.

Grandma's Wicker Rocking Chair
by Joan (Michalke) Ritchey

In my idle hours when
My mind is free to wander
I travel back in time with
Memories to ponder.

Grandma's wicker rocking chair
Sits empty and alone
No longer does it rock
To her sweet melodic tone.

Grandpa bought the chair for Grandma in 1898
When their first child was born
She rocked the lad to sleep at night
And at nap times in the morn.

Five more children were to come
Into Gram and Grandpa's life
Hard times were spent in Iowa
For the farmer and his wife.

In 1920, news from Oregon
Spoke of greener pastures there
"Leaving family and friends," said Grandma
"Was hard for me to bear."

The worn and treasured rocker
Was the first thing on the moving van.
Carefully the piece was placed
For the long cross-country span.

Tears were shed at leaving
And continued along the dusty road,
The final good-bye was at the cemetery
For their first-born's death (at four years old).

They found a spot by a sunny window
On the farm in Forest Grove
Where the wicker rocker took its place
In the parlor room alcove.

Soon Grandma resumed her rocking
And softly sang her lullabies
This time to her grandchildren
Soothing aches, and pains, and cries.

Many years have passed since then,
I own Grandma's wicker rocking chair
And gazing upon the cherished antique
I envision Grandma seated there.

His Mistake

From our in-home real estate office I watched an unfamiliar, older white van pull up to my shop, then slowly back up to turn around. The driver stopped, got out, and walked into my always-open three-bay machine shed. He came back out a minute later lugging something.

Something of mine!

For several weeks during July and August, the rural neighborhood west of Forest Grove had been victimized by a half-dozen bold, daylight robberies. A nondescript beat-up white van, with the last three license numbers 919, had been reported to be the vehicle used by the thief. This was a gripping concern in our rural community because on one occasion a spaced-out robber confronted a young mother and her home-schooled children with a knife. That doper guy was brazen and vicious!

I went to the closet by our front door and grabbed my ancient over-and-under shotgun rifle that I'd inherited from my grandfather. Then I stepped out onto our front porch—*the thief had to drive back past our house to exit our country place.*

The driver slowly pulled away from the machine shed

and came down our driveway. The van looked like it had spent most of its unhappy automobile life on the Oregon coast, judging by the peeling orange rust. I held up my arm signaling for him to stop and then chambered a shell into the quaint, double-barreled gun. The metallic click was highly audible in the lethargic, muggy air.

I raised my arm more forcefully... still no hesitation by the van driver. Then my eye caught the last three numbers of the license plate—919! *It was him!*

He had probably figured we weren't home during the day.

Through the open van window, I saw a flash of metal. *Was he armed?*

He began to accelerate!

I took quick aim and put a rifle shot just over the top rear of his vehicle.

Then he really floor-boarded that old Ford Econoline van! A gusty cloud of oily black smoke shot out the rear and the back tires churned rocks on our graveled driveway.

I levered in another rifle shell and shot into his front tire! I heard a metallic ping as the hollow-point bullet hit both metal and rubber. Then a resounding pop!

Rapidly changing barrels, I fired the 12-gauge shotgun into the rear of his rusty van, shattering one window. The smell of gunpowder was pungent in the still air. I heard his front tire rim clunking on the gravel.

The blocky shaped vehicle then veered to the right, edging close to my half-acre fishpond. There's just a scant few feet between our driveway and the pond, and a steep bank drops off into the reservoir. The old van slowly slipped into the deepest water and because of the open and blasted out windows, it began taking on water like a mini Titanic.

I heard him scream, "Son of a bitch!" as the van submerged.

By damn! It looked like 919s robbing days were over.

I don't believe I have an ingrained mean streak, but I sure was hoping the man couldn't swim.

The Turd-Wagon Wars

The overzealous tenant came tearing out of the manufactured rental house. He was hollering and shouting. The "wagon" pulled onto the rural site, loaded with its odorous portable Schultz toilet, and had stopped next to the Christmas trees. The driver, Mike Hepler, expertly jockeyed the wagon onto a level spot below the driveway that led to the rental house. Next, he quickly unhooked his pickup to access the large water tank used for weed spraying, which was located on the pickup bed. Then the turd-wagon *fun* really got started as two cars of Latino workers pulled up and parked adjacent to the pickup. The men slowly got out of the cars and lazily stretched after their hour-long ride.

The tenant apparently considered the Schultz site to be part of his rental domain, even if that area technically wasn't on his property. There was just no way he would be forced to gaze upon the obnoxious outhouse. Tempers flared on both sides.

The Latino workers watched the heated verbal exchange with stoic good humor. And the tenant's family inside the house cheered loudly for Dad.

Now as Schultz toilets go, this portable unit was an elite model—clean and shiny new. Almost pristine and highly polished! It certainly was not objectionable by most standards except for the common, "Not in my backyard" attitude.

Mike, the driver, was irritated. He wanted to get the Latino crew to work and he became increasingly animated. "Mexicans have to go to the bathroom too!" he said. "Would you rather see them mooning you off in the brush?"

The tenant replied, "Well, no, but this is my front yard and my whole family looks out here!"

"We need a level place and we'll be here for only one day. And besides, you'll soon be leaving for work anyway," Mike said.

The tense scene turned into a genuine Mexican standoff. The red-faced tenant shouted, "I'm going to call the landlord!"

Mike shot back, "I'll call him, too!"

At home, I received both phone calls and remained calm. I've learned not to initially over-react, just to listen so I can hear everyone's side. I encouraged them to say whatever was on their mind, to just spill their guts. I suppose it's rather like a confessional. So I listened to the tenant, and commented in a consoling, but hopefully not condescending manner, all the while trying to suppress a chuckle. Although, I confess, I could not hold back a smile.

I told the tenant we really, really appreciated his "pride of ownership" on our place, but the Christmas tree work had to be done to improve their quality. And besides, we did not need a Tex/Mex Alamo re-run in Oregon.

Next, the call came in from Mike, the wagon driver, who was surprisingly calm by then, and I heard him out. Then he and I discussed one or two other less obtrusive sites for the Schultz. But the less objectionable sites were further away, so would require more walking. And with eight hombres working by the hour, time *is* money. *Oh well, what's new*, I thought.

So everybody's pulse got back into the normal range, I think. Just a typical fun, fun day as a rural land-and-not lord!

And now the Christmas tree market has plummeted so low that we can't even give the daggone trees away.

Licking The Bowl

Probably you think I'm talking about a starving dog or a six o'clock in the evening mewing pussycat. My ten-year-old well-fed "puppy" still slicks her bowl and my wife, Joan, and I occasionally joke about letting special girl Banner dog tongue-wash all the evening dishes. But, no, I'm *not* talking about four-legged animals.

One of my earliest memories was watching an aunt use her index finger to lick the bowl with the pretense of, "Just checking the flavor," but she was really getting every last little smidgen of food. I also must admit that aunt was so doggone tight that she squeaked like a rusty piece of farm equipment. But… whenever the stars properly aligned, licking the stirring spoon became my savory chore.

"Waste not, want not," was *preached* and *practiced* in our family. I believe our Scottish genes were doing their duty, and often it was double duty. The partially cooked potato peelings were fed to the sows and I can still see Mom chugging out to the barn, me slowly trailing along, lugging a partial pail of other vegetable scraps. Buckets of pig treat happened often enough that the big ole mama sows would wait right next to the gate. Then I'd watch the hogs go ape for all those tasty morsels. Sometimes now I think the pigs' ancestors came from that cold, Scot part of the world too. I suppose the pigs' addiction could have started with all those spoiled spuds during the Potato Famine.

But, the real "life lessons" came in relation to the almighty dollar! This nitty-gritty subject was where reliable Goodrich rubber met the road, especially on my maternal side in the Nichols-McCue family. Two of my uncles balanced their ledgers books—an accounting of all income and expenses to the penny *every single night*. Mom did her reckoning only once a week, but her tallying included five cents spent for gum, fifteen cents for a whatcha-ma-ding, and ten dollars for hair styling, or twelve dollars and fifty-nine cents for gas. If the books did not balance, neither heaven nor hell rested comfortably until they did! After considerable time spent pouring over her books and not getting them to jive, Mom would call her brother and ask him to come over for financial accounting help. They both had the need to arrive at that absolutely necessary zero balance! None of the family was a "plugger," (bookkeepers who insert any old number, just to make it balance.)

Most of their lessons stuck with me. I still stoop to pick up a lonely penny, usually all wet or dirty with tire marks. I must be getting to be a rare breed, because I find one every week, plus skinny dimes, or even the occasional fat nickel. I don't find many quarters however, perhaps because they are worth gutter-diving for in this protracted recession.

Now you may not believe this, but through the years, I've found a lot of money. The largest wad was two thousand dollars I found in—of all places—the vault of a local Forest Grove bank. The money had been missing for several hours and sweat had started forming on the brows of a few tellers. The packet of hundred dollar bills was tucked in the corner of the podium in the vault. And I didn't even get a reward! And just last week, I found fifty dollars in wet soggy bills in a hedge. I think I found the owner, but she said I could keep it, but I won't.

The biggest dilemma I've had recently was in San Diego at the airport when Joan and I were waiting to catch a cruise ship. Joan's sister and brother-in-law met us there for a short visit. I needed to visit the urinal, which was a real busy place to hang out. And guess what was in the urinals? Why, great stars in the morning! Each one of those pissers was chock full of change AND almost all appeared to be quarters. There were six urinals and my internal math calculator was going bonkers, I guessed the total would have more than filled a kid's big fat pink piggy bank!

I know I came out of there with dollar signs in my eyes, so my brother-in-law, who is also a frugal guy, shot into that restroom for verification, not knowing I don't lie about nitty-gritty stuff like that.

So we devised a plan to reconnoiter some rubber or latex gloves from a cleaning lady. One trouble was the steady flow of gentlemen into the bathroom. I was amazed that no one else showed a spark of interest in the huge potential gain. I know each commode had at least enough change to buy two packs of today's expensive cigarettes, or a six-pack of some high-priced suds. Further, hands can be washed. Right?

Talking about suds remind me of another rank tale from long ago. This tale supposedly took place in Klamath Falls at a college dormitory. A drinking party was taking place and one of the guys involved was known to be a freeloader—he would never chip in to buy the beer. So after he'd helped himself to several bottles, the rest of the bunch filled up one bottle with... yep, you guessed it... frothy, yellow piss, which he apparently gulped down, mentioned afterward that it tasted a little salty.

But back to the San Diego Airport story...

Double-darn, our plane's imminent departure short-circuited that rubber-glove plan, so all I can do is just speculate about what could have been. Maybe I should carry a pair of latex gloves when I travel. You know I already pack a good supply of Vaseline....

144

Commonality

The oldest two... were not a pair to draw in
Sisters, one uglier than all of sin
One beautiful by most standards
Their commonness was
The liberally inherited mean streak
That had sucked
Their thin gentleness dry

I got to know the third younger sister
She became an in-law
Somehow, they cross
All lines of sensibility
Sadly, she got a giant dose, too
Of the family meanness gene
They had learned well
That their spiteful words
Could cut like a sword

The ugly one never married
She had nothing to offer
Other than a patronizing smile
And always looking for someone to sue

The youngest was oversexed
And would have been the village whore
In earlier times

Attempting many conquests
With anything that wore pants
This habit blamed
On a sailor guy
From her youthful days
No one bought that story either

And the beautiful one
Why she had this raw, bitchy,
Always-complaining personality
Her husband died young
Just to get shut of her.

The Oil-less Bloodbath

She was impossible to miss! The young woman was a
sloppy, obese person standing next to a beater car with its
door hanging open. That rusty, older vehicle was parked a
couple of stalls over from our work pickup, strangely
backed into the parking space kept for apartment visitors.
She appeared jumpy or nervous and glanced furtively
about as she ground out a half-smoked cigarette longer
than a whores' dream.

A somewhat newer, but terribly battered pickup was
parked on the other side of the woman's car. That truck
had also backed in and was partially full of household
items, which made me assume someone was moving. I
thought, *Lucky them,* because I hate moving. Neither vehicle
had been there when we'd arrived an hour earlier to begin
pruning trees on our adjacent duplex rental. A thought
crossed my mind. *If they were moving, why didn't they park
closer to the apartment?*

Our rental's location was not in a good neighborhood,
and to call it unsavory would have been kind. My partner,
Ron Wade, and I had acquired this property, which
included a vacant lot, at an incredibly low price, anticipating

that the projected light rail construction would change the dollar landscape. But until that magical slipper danced, we simply had to deal with the resident scuzzballs next door. The large apartment complex had more than two hundred units.

Cleaning debris from the vacant lot was something we had to continually address, and that unhappy chore really ticked off my partner. But that day we were addressing the trees and shrubs that overhung our duplex. I went to fetch more chainsaw oil from our pickup, which had a canopy cover and a utility trailer attached. The pickup was parked behind the garage of our duplex.

I unlocked the pickup canopy to grab the quart of chainsaw oil. Just then, another woman, very skinny, and two raunchy-looking guys came scurrying around the back of the apartment building. The woman carried a plastic bag and the guys had several objects they quickly placed into the back of their pickup.

The can of chainsaw oil had rolled three-fourths of the way forward in the bed of pickup, making it necessary for me to climb into the bed to retrieve it. I was in the awkward act of extending my body forward under the windowed canopy when the three headed towards me. I thought, *Uh, oh.*

The skinny woman said in a smart-ass sneer, "Well, and what do we have here?"

I nonchalantly responded, "Just grabbing some chainsaw oil." I noticed all four had sweaty sheens on their faces, but it was not a warm day.

A look passed between the skinny woman and one guy and he said in a nasal voice, "We can help you."

Making another quick up and down read on them, I was already dang sure it would be the wrong kind of help. They crowded in closer to me, increasing my apprehension.

Ron, my partner, was on the front-side of the flat duplex roof with our new pole chainsaw. The roof height allowed us to reach and cut some of the higher tree limbs. I wondered, *Can he hear any of this conversation?* So I spoke louder, "NO, I DON'T NEED YOUR HELP."

At about that point it thudded home. I had probably interrupted a robbery. I could feel my already damaged heart start to race and go out of control. And then another scary thought dawned on me that this foursome was probably on something—some drug—based on their spacey, drawn looks and their rotten and missing teeth. The two rascally men and the skinny woman were greedily eyeing the expensive tools I'd stashed in our pickup truck. One of the guys tried to push me as I hastily backed away, and the other smiled maliciously as he pulled out a switchblade knife. The skinny woman, who seemed to be the leader, popped her gum with a loud smack and said, "Give us your keys."

The situation had fast changed into an extremely dangerous confrontation, and either their drug-induced state or their need for money—probably both—convinced them I was easy pickings. It was scary apparent to me that this quartet had a habit of victimizing the unwary, the old, and the disabled.

I laboriously hopped over the trailer tongue and grabbed a fold-up hand-pruning saw from our tool rack on the trailer. I pushed the blade release and the foot-long blade sprang open. For a nanosecond, I felt like Crocodile Dundee. But, there were still four of them to just one of me—and me with the diagnosis of a heart attack waiting to happen.

I thought, *No pickup or tools are worth my life, so just toss them the keys.* But, no! I couldn't. Those top-of-the-line Stihl tools and the pickup were a big part of our livelihood, some not yet paid for. I ran to the end of the trailer. The two guys slowly followed me, stalking like cats, sure of their prey and obviously enjoying their advantage. The tension ratcheted up! The woman gum smacker said, "Hurry it up," to her cohorts.

Then I heard the most welcome sound, the buzz of our fully revved pole chainsaw! But the chain was howling at a high-pitched whine because the oil reservoir was empty.

Ron came tearing around the end of the garage right at the two guys beside the trailer. He fenced with the guy who had the switchblade, and then rapidly jabbed the pole saw between the guy's legs and started to tilt the end up higher towards his crotch.

Everything came to a standstill except the revved up pole saw. Fear was written all over the face of the guy straddling the chainsaw, but he was still gripping the switchblade. He seemed momentarily frozen, probably shocked by the rapid shift of circumstance. I also had the impression that the gum-chewing woman handled the man's heavy thinking.

Ron inched the screeching chain higher, then turned the saw on a slight angle and took out a piece of the guy's Levi jeans. Then more, a lot more. Blood was lubricating the chain. The robber shrieked and finally dropped the switchblade as he grabbed the side of trailer to hold himself up.

I advanced on the other punk with my hand-pruning saw. He backed up to the end of our ladders and I firmly laid the saw teeth on his arm and started to rake backwards, immediately drawing several pinpricks of blood. Ron threatened this guy with a slight move of the pole saw and the man made a motion as if he was giving up.

I hollered, "Get into the trailer bed and lie down!"

The switchblade guy was screaming, moaning, and cursing all at once. He grabbed his profusely bleeding leg with both hands and began to fold over onto the blood-spattered ground.

The woman leader headed for the car. The obese lookout had already climbed in. Ron ran to the front of the vehicle and rammed the still-running pole saw through the plastic grill and into the radiator. Antifreeze coated the pole saw, diluting the blood.

We heard sirens approaching—apparently, someone driving into the parking lot noticed the melee and called 911. I felt my heart drop back into a more normal range.

It turned out that the thieves lived in the huge apartment complex, at the far end. The apartments they'd been ransacking included one occupied by a long-time apartment maintenance man, who had recently died. That fellow had been well liked and the robbers figured many apartment residents would attend his funeral. They just hadn't figured on being the lubricant for a chainsaw.

Me And The Screwed Up Rooster

The cocky rooster must have hatched this spring and now strongly feels the need to flaunt his stuff and practice crowing for the rest of the flock. The earliest I've heard him is at the screwed-up time of 1:30 a.m. His crow is coming from somewhere off in the Dilley distance, pretending dawn is arriving somewhere, and then sneaking over the hen house roof. I'd guess many of my neighbors think he is good candidate for the hatchet. Maybe the proud, but sleepless owners are training him for the annual Canby Cock Crowing Contest.

I can relate to this fouled up fowl. My sleep clock is severely screwed up, too. Enough to where my wife, Joan, has started asking "Is something the matter?" We both know that something is the matter. The real question though is—how many layers deep?

Oh, the poor dog follows me around when the owls are hooting and the dingy rooster is crowing. But thankfully, Banner is capable of napping anywhere, just like her sleep-deprived and slightly depraved sometimes master.

Lately, the messed up rooster starts his show promptly at four a.m. Like Pavarotti, he is in full throat immediately, with a cocky crow every ten or twelve seconds. So I have concluded he was raised in Nova Scotia, or perhaps neighboring Newfoundland, then somehow migrated and is now integrating our little spot of previous peace and quiet. Maybe he saw the movie, *One Flew over the Cuckoo's Nest*, and decided Oregon is the place he should be.

The crowing began long before the Daylight Saving Time switcheroo. God bless Ben Franklin and his idea to save street light costs. (Why do we always seek someone or something to blame?)

No, this time I think I'll choose retirement as the recipient of my blame game. My "flex" hours allow me to nap with great spontaneity and I take full advantage of this oldster perk. Amazingly, I can fall asleep in the middle of a sentence. I need no excuse—even what starts out as a wink can just put me under, anywhere, anytime, and anyplace.

I do get to—as you can tell—act out my compulsion to write while in my foggy state of mind. But this mental scribbling is a real challenge as I drift in and out of a sleepy stupor.

Retirement also provides the privilege of putting my ear to the window and listening for crickets. (Strangely, crickets are still chirping out there, and today is November 10, and we've just had four inches of rain.) I'm doing scientific research for a story on crickets, so now its roosters, crickets, and hot chocolate in the wee, wee hours.

The Misnomer

December solstice is
A misnomer
The changing of the guard
From the fall season to winter
So the calendars say
Always too late
In the annual cycle
We have already felt
The cold breath of arctic winds
Sleet has pounded our face
The creeks are running a banker
Our nights are never ending
The elk have stopped bugling
Sundown is at four p.m.
Its rays are weak and puny
Not full and proud as in July
All the summer birds
Long ago joined the migratory trek
The chipmunks are in their den
My hands are all a-tingle
So mittens are at hand
I know my toes are next
Thank God for electric blankets
To partially protect me
From my wife's exploring feet.

The Pumpkin Ridge Fire & Other Scary Blazes

Fires, with their billowing gray or black smoke, were just part of life growing up in western Oregon where Mr. Douglas Fir reigned as the king tree. We had woodstoves at home, set slash fires on our property, and used fire to burn out stumps when we cleared fields just like our ancestors had done for centuries. And of course, Native Indians had occasionally started fires to increase open areas for better hunting. Fires seemed more noticeable in rural hinterlands during the 1930s and 1940s when I was a boy. Maybe because fire-fighting equipment was extremely limited.

THE TILLAMOOK BURN

Doug Fir is stronger than steel, but it was nothing against the Tillamook Burn that consumed thousands of acres of pristine trees. The Tillamook Burn was actually a series of forest fires in what is now known as the Tillamook State Forest. The fires took place between 1933 and 1951, and destroyed 355,000 miles of old growth timber.

I saw—and smelled—the oppressive, rolling smoke of the 1945 Tillamook Burn as it circled around our property for weeks. The smoke had funneled high into the sky and traveled for thousands of miles before dissipating. Debris was deposited on ships more than 500 miles out to sea. The 1945 fire was visible from Highway 6 and 26, the routes from Portland to the coast. Some of the kids I went to school with saw actual flames from their homes in the nearby communities of Timber, Cochran, and Gales Creek.

Three of my classmates were from the Lyda family whose logging operation reportedly started one of the three biggest of the Tillamook Burns. And, strangely, the fires happened every six years—in 1933, 1939, 1945, and 1951, but the last one was relatively small, regarding acreage burned.

To the best of my recollection, the Lyda brothers were logging on a very hot summer afternoon, dragging a big log to be cut and loaded. They shut down for the day, but later, the friction of dragging the monster log started smoldering then caught fire during the night. Apparently, by morning the flames were racing through the tops of trees faster than a horse could run.

That type of blaze is called a crown fire. One of the oddities of a crown fire is that often many smaller trees below are untouched, and sometimes an entire canyon will luckily be missed by these racing fires. This happens because the wind can make a fire jump great distances. The most aggressive crown fire destroyed the forest at the rate of 21 square miles per hour in some of the best timber the world has ever known.

Many high school kids between 1945 and the 1970s helped replant the terribly devastated burned areas. In fact, two of my best friends worked in the timber industry and helped replant an area several miles west of Forest Grove. Forty years later, one of them, Dale Zumwalt, was back on the same exact site to thin some of "his" trees because they had grown to a commercial diameter and made fine logs. Those trees had grown at least 42 inches a year, which is what occurs on a Class I forest site. But they were second growth so did not have the desirable close annual ring count of true old growth fir.

FIRE AT HOME

Our little family of four burned wood in a huge furnace located in our full basement. The furnace door measured 16-x-16 inches, with a proportional size firebox. It easily kept the farmhouse warm all night, even in the frigid part of the year as long as Dad chucked it full at bedtime. Our home, built in 1936, did not have a smidgen of insulation, just lath and plastered walls, and thick, machined cedar shake siding. We also had a kitchen woodstove and even a dumbwaiter with pulleys to bring the wood upstairs from the basement for Mom's woodstove. When I was old enough, I filled in for that dumb waiter on a regular basis just because I was a bit faster. I remember thinking my sister was far more qualified than I was to stand in for the "dumb" part of the dumbwaiter.

Every fall precipitated the raking of leaves—moving them to a big pile—and then the ritual of setting gigantic bonfires. Mom was always a part of this ritual because she liked fire, and because my mom was not a slacker. I also remember several times when her brother, Wilby, visited from Minnesota and helped big time while on his vacation. Wilby and my Uncle Dwight both loved burning stuff.

FARM FIELD CLEARING

Every fall and winter during the slack times on the Ritchey Brothers farm, our crew of eight, counting us boy kids and the hired men, would tackle tree and brush removal on a field we planned to cultivate. The fields' sizes ranged from ten acres to perhaps forty. My family had been clearing new pieces of virgin timber ground almost every year since arriving in Oregon in the spring of 1920. We cut the marketable trees for timber, and "junk" logs for firewood, then would trim the logs and pile the brush.

Junk trees in those times were any tree other than fir or cedar. Do you know what a Swede saw is? Or a brush hook? No? Well, the Swede saw has a stiff elongated U-shaped metal frame with a very thin sharp-toothed blade. It is a one-man saw (because two Swedes like to argue too much, ha, ha). A two-man saw would have a six- or eight-foot length and be called a "crosscut." A brush hook has a heavy curved blade sharpened just like an axe. Those were common tools for many, many years and I have experienced a blister or two from their hickory handles. My uncle, Paul Ritchey, was as slick as they come for hitting the spot he aimed at. I always figured he would have done pretty darn good at our Washington County Fair hitting that gong thing and getting his choice of a pretty doll for a prize. Of course, it helped to have a pile-driving rear end for making that gong go off.

It always seemed like the Fourth of July when we'd blow the field stumps sky high using several sticks of dynamite. We just had to make darn sure the fuse was long enough. One time we were blowing stumps on the Johnson Place, but those stumps were rooted in a mucky clay area. My Uncle Curtis, who usually set the dynamite, had already lit the fuses and was running back through the thick gumbo mud to safety. First, he lost one knee boot, and then the other, but he sure wasn't slowing down or stopping.

After the dynamiting, it was time to start picking up thousands of roots because the roots could mess up a grain drill or combine. The size of these roots ranged from six inches to six feet. Sometimes the root hunks were so heavy, us kids could not manage them so one of the handy grownups would grab a hold and do a bit of man-grunting. To me, it sometimes seemed as though this picking up of the blasted roots went on forever because in general, a field required at least three pickings—three times bending, stooping, and throwing or carrying.

Our family had a specially designed low flatbed trailer we used to pile the roots on. The trailer was pulled by our D2 Cat, which on flat ground could be set and stay straight for a long ways without any driver. In between each of the three pickings, we would run a piece of equipment with big C curved teeth to bring more roots to the surface. These huge dumping-pile fires of fir, maple, or oak root wads would burn for days. Twice every day Uncle Curtis—on our Allis-Chambers bulldozer—would push the remains together. Talk about a gigantic weenie roast! We had a lot of burnt "buns" too.

ANOTHER CLOSE CALL

My cousin, Gary, and I very nearly started a forest fire while cutting fireplace wood to sell to Hugh McGilvra—we had a prearranged deal with him. Hugh was the owner of the *Forest Grove News Times*, and his son, Paul, was in the same grade as me. Paul helped with some of the woodcutting and we all earned points for a completed Boy Scout project. This "almost" fire disaster story, "The Tendrils," was included in my first book, *Hankering For The*

Way It Was. That potential calamity still makes my stomach churn.

I was thoroughly cognizant of fire danger because of that earlier incident, plus all my Cub Scout and Boy Scout training with Morrie Hines. We've all read about people torching themselves while messing with gasoline or other flammables. Gasoline literally explodes when pitched on an open flame, and so you'd better not have the gas trailing back to you *or* to a container sitting too close when you strike a match. Probably though, my best teaching came from home by observing and learning from cautious folks.

PUMPKIN RIDGE FIRE

The Pumpkin Ridge potential catastrophe episode took place when I was in my early forties. We, meaning my two partners and I, were logging a forty-acre patch of nice Doug Fir timber on a short dead-end road that hooked up to Pumpkin Ridge, the main road. The site was about eight miles northwest of North Plains, considered the "boonies" back then. I think Pumpkin Ridge Road whelped more wannabe outlaws then downtown Portland, especially in those years. And I know that here are a lot of bodies up there that will never be found.

We had already cut, hauled, and sold the bulk of some top-notch, export timber from the acreage and were cleaning up around the very comfortable house we intended to rent to some nice family. "Comfortable" in this case means the house was a brick single-level on five acres. Brick houses were an oddity on the Ridge in those times— long before the Pumpkin Ridge Golf Course idea was kicked loose. That Ridge area is almost respectable now, at least in some areas.

Anyway, we were being highly selective with our falling and just removing a few trees scattered around the house so that home site would not look scalped. This was in the fall of the year. There had already been two or three good soaking rains and another weather front was just coming in. The slash and debris fire appeared to be burning safely, so we let the two small piles burn down and spaded around them. By then, the rain was falling fairly hard and so we pulled out for home, feeling reasonably secure about the lack of danger.

But... *surprise, surprise, surprise!*

It was four days later and the fall weather temperature had spiked up high. I answered the first call from the North Plains Fire Department and was told they had been called out to fight a fire on our little operation. I confirmed that we had permits to cut and burn up there and so we were all legal—we always were on those logging and replanting deals. I admit I push the envelope in some situations, but I love trees and probably have planted ten times as many as any tree hugger.

Then I got the second call, this from the rural fire fighters. So both the city Fire Department and the rural responders went tearing up that snaky, winding Pumpkin Ridge Road. The rural department had smaller trucks, which were better for driving off-road. Sirens were screaming and echoing through the canyons, which we learned later from the neighbors.

I'd gotten the call because my name was first on the permit, so I immediately tried to let my two partners know about the fix we were in. They were both working their weekday jobs—Dale Zumwalt had been hauling logs since three a.m., and Ron was working in the concrete business with me, trying to appraise some piece of real estate.

We were in a frenzy. All three of us were worried and calling back and forth. Then five long, ulcer-starting hours later, a good news call came in. Almost everything was okay. No significant damage except a few more trees had fallen. They had drenched the area and said an old retired guy nearby was still out checking every little bit on the site.

Apparently, our "safe" fire had smoldered in the ground on a root and then grown into an active blaze. *We were lucky!* Still, we had to pay for the healthy fine and got a little talking to by the guy with a Ranger hat. He allowed as how we had done most things correctly, but that we should have had someone monitor the burn, especially when the temperature shot up.

Graceful And Pert

Mighty fir limbs
Always an attraction for me
My eyes are drawn like a magnet
The tree length and shape
Inspires my breath
And the mother tree
Strikes the tone of what shall be

Some firs gracefully cascade
Like a gentle mountain slope
Others are pert and sassy
Like a maiden's breast
We see them from afar
Their lovely profiles outlined
Against any sky

The Act

He was the greatest
The greatest
Of the high wire acts
It was not just a show
His very life depended
On his nimble feet
Combined with incredible balance
It wasn't just
The big payoff
For walking the high wire
There was the thrill
Always the thrill of performing
And the local audience
Cheering him on
For his very life
Hung in the balance
More in *his* balance
Such bravery exhibited
There was not a net
We always applauded
Joy written on our faces
As the little
Red squirrel
Climbed down the pole
And dropped safely to the ground.

The Three Rs

"I am not going to pay you guys!" I said.

It didn't take a brain surgeon to gauge their disappointed reactions. My opening statement was not one hundred percent accurate, but poking fun is one way to open *my* gate. Besides, joshing livens up everyone's life.

But, quicker than a cat, the dumb situation escalated. Then I jumped on my Irish Soapbox (which I've been known to do now and then) and said, "What are you guys learning in school?"

This was the second frustrating day after I'd hired two young squirts to help me with odd jobs around our seven back-achy acres. One of the teenage boys was a grandson of my long-time friend and helper, Philemon Ortiz. This grandson was a freshman in high school, and his friend and future brother-in-law was a sophomore. I say *future brother-in-law* because the older kid was old enough to get an erection, which I guess we can joke about now because of the saturation of Viagra advertisements on television. (I call them stallion ads.)

Anyway, the sophomore had fathered a child with Philemon's granddaughter at his ripe old age of thirteen.

The girl was fifteen. But, that's another, even more gut-wrenching story that gets my Irish up and I won't go into it here, or perhaps ever.

Well, these two kids had each worked for me a total of seven hours in two days. The three of us had agreed that seven dollars cash per hour was in the ballpark for a fair wage. The per hour dollar amount was without a doubt overpay for the younger kid 'cause he liked to flap his jaws, but both of them were slower than molasses in a Wisconsin winter. And the kids together didn't even equal one-half of their sixty-five year old grandpa's work stamina. But, I was determined to help my friend, Philemon, teach them how to get up a sweat.

As I drove the two boys home on that particular day, I asked them once more, "How much do I owe you?" Only silence, which I interpreted as confusion on their part. I made this assumption due to the quick glances back and forth between them as I watched their faces in my rearview mirror.

So I repeated their doomsday payday ultimatum again, but more forcefully. "I am not going to pay you guys until you tell me what I owe you! What is seven hours times seven dollars?"

Then, they started guessing—mostly the older one. The younger one kept his mouth shut, so as to not display even more ignorance. This wild guessing went on for several minutes—the time it took to drive five miles in average traffic. I heard almost every number in the thirties, forties, fifties, and sixties—except the right one.

It was also obvious that no one had taught them, *When an uneven number is multiplied by an uneven number, the number on the right, or the single digit column, has to be uneven!*

I was clenching my teeth, trying to keep control of myself, but I failed. And when I get disturbed, cuss words can erupt from my three-quarter Irish mouth. I know, I know, swearing is a deplorable habit, but those two knot-heads were testing my hard-won, battle-scarred, old-age patience, a characteristic that had obviously been short-circuited in my Grandpa McCue. His flaw had rolled into me in a direct conduit through my mom, and patience has sometimes been in short supply during my three-score plus fifteen winters.

Several "centuries" later, while we were parked in front of their residence, the kids still did not have the correct answer. I was in absolute total disbelief! And the question kept forming in my mind, What is taking place in our school system? I think I knew the answer.

So... I hatched a plan to maybe work them through this life-learning, simple math problem. I asked, "What is seven times ten?"

"Seventy," the older one answered.

Whew, I breathed. Next question, "What is seventy minus seven?" A little hesitation…

"Sixty-three."

Then I asked, "What is sixty-three minus seven?" This toughie created mass consternation and confusion on both faces but finally, after a couple of guesses, as I continued to swear under my breath, I heard a questioning, "Fifty-six?"

"So, okay," I said. "What is fifty-six minus seven?"

The sophomore almost shouted, "Forty-nine!" And the younger kid mouthed it, too, pretending like he was right there on the same page.

All three of us were so delirious, you would have thought we discovered America.

"Holy crap!" I crowed, "You two are not going to be cheated today." Then I paid them, and made them COUNT THEIR CASH.

Finally, I let them out of my car.

I needed a LONG nap when I got home.

A Terrible Master

I stared long and hard at the three potential renters. For some reason their mouths were slightly agape and I could see what remained of their horribly discolored teeth. I don't think there was a full complement of thirty-two teeth among the three of them. And for damn sure, none of them had any "wisdom" molars. Stringy, long, greasy hair framed their Neanderthal countenances.

I was standing close enough to detect a putrid odor. Rotten teeth and dirty hair smell like something going bad. I backed away, but the odor clung to me as if it had made a home in my nose.

The interview improved with each dismal nanosecond. This trio had been our only rental applicants in almost three months, and we were already forty-five days late with our mortgage payment.

They said they had the "grease"—the cash—for the deposit and first month's rent. Their roll of greenbacks had already been flashed. Worse, I knew where and *what* the stash had come from. The members of the trio were friends of a school acquaintance of mine, and she was hooked, too. Whoring was her game.

I knew the path that had led me by the nose—greed. Greed is a terrible master—your relatives don't like you, not even at Christmas. I think greed starts at a very early age with snacks, toys and envy—lots of envy—then too often getting your way.

I've known a few kids who got spoiled and at least one of their parents were very deliberate about doing it. One even stated to me, "Well, she's our last and so I guess we can spoil her!" I've heard other reasons and you have too. The result is predictable—that child will struggle to survive in the real world.

Gray On *Gray*...

She gradually ... became form
Allowed by a thin wind
Piercing yellow eyes fixed on two objects
First, her primary prey,
Then me

The dense fog was blanketing
Water dripping like rain
The slight breeze was blowing
From me to her
So ... she had known

Of my presence
But her hunger
And demanding pups
Pushed relentlessly
For food

I retreated
To hopefully allow
Her seizure of the rodent
Then came
The long, graceful pounce

The audible snap
A muted tiny shrill
And violent shake
To snap
The gopher's brown neck

Another glance at me
With those yellow eyes
And perhaps
A look of triumph,
Purely primordial

She turned to me
Once more
Then was again
Wrapped in fog
Gray on gray

We became friends
In a remote way
Through her morning ritual
That included a pass
Through apple trees and green meadow

Then the neighbor
Playing the Big White Hunter
A single shot
Destroyed the den

Gray on gray...

Motley

I watched the crummy old Dodge pickup idle up beside me at the stoplight. I suppose its dented, rusty condition caught my eye. My sporty red Toyota SUV height allowed me way too good a view of the crap strewn in the back of the pickup. A large, beat up tool chest was sitting at an angle, along with a rusty push lawnmower. Empty pop cans, Big Mac paper cups, grass clippings, assorted tools, used paint cans, and a double-compartment kitchen sink was under the rest of the mess.

The driver sported a motley-colored reddish gray beard and mustache—but no, I'm not sure the scraggly facial hair even reached that lowly motley category. A pencil-thin long brown cigarette dangled from the corner of his compressed lips, and an earring decorated his left ear. I'm still so dumb on that stuff that I do not know the meaning of what left or right ear hangings, but perhaps the men wearing earrings don't know either. Oh, yeah, I almost forgot—an elongated blue penis was tattooed on his left arm. It was real hard to miss, even with my ancient eyeballs.

The light changed in the super slow traffic and the beater pickup eased alongside two guys revving their oil-smoking, hotrod engine—which struck me as strange since they were driving a fairly new deep maroon PT cruiser convertible. The driver kept pressing the throttle of the PT to squeal his fancy whitewall tires, just to get everyone's attention. Then I spotted a red bulbous nose and a golden can of liquid being tipped up to his ~~bulbous~~ huge lips, causing his ~~huge~~ Adam's apple to bob rhythmically as some of the liquid missed his mouth and dribbled onto his naked chest.

Do you ever wonder why that throat bump got tagged as Adam's apple? Why not John's plum? And why is it that the folks with large apples almost always have extra long necks?

Anyhow, the Adam's apple driver turned sideways and grunted something to what appeared to be a close brethren, judging by the same huge throat protrusion, floppy lips, hair color and matching beaked nose. For sure, those two retreads came from the same litter!

The Cruiser guy, too, had spotted the old pickup with all the crap in back. His inbred buddy in the passenger seat guffawed something, then tipped down more fortified eight-percent stuff for proper emphasis and had the good sense to heave his partially full can of suds towards the beater pickup. Beer and foam sprayed Motley as it zipped by. Then the can hit the metal behind the window and landed in the back of the pickup to join the clutter.

Motley let out a mighty oath and swerved slightly. The

young hotrod driver got even more stupid, and flipped the universal bird sign, setting the stage for a good road rage ruckus between a Red Neck and a couple of punks.

Unbeknownst to the two punks, Motley had a large and mature German shepherd lying beside the old tool chest. The dog reared up, his ears forming erect points as the beer can clanged around in the pickup bed. He heard his master's vehement swearing and positioned himself in a ready crouch. Surprisingly, the mostly black dog looked as good as everything else looked bad! He was the picture of good health and tender care with his shiny dark coat on a well fed frame. Apparently, Motley did some things right.

Then we were braking for another light and the punks' idea of fun definitely headed for the South Pole. I heard Motley say, "Get 'em!"

That beautiful shepherd easily cleared the span into the back of the PT Cruiser convertible, and before you could blink, he was reefing on the ear of the second punk. It could have been a pig's ear, judging from all the oinking going on.

Then Motley rammed his rusty pickup into the side of the Cruiser. Thick metal from the 1970s scraped and screeched against the vastly inferior alloys of the modern car. He also flicked his burning cigarette onto the lap of the driver. Motley then whistled his big, beautiful shepherd back to the pickup bed. The brutal ramming forced the Punks' car over to the curb and onto the sidewalk, right smack into a fancy new street light. The crash was quite audible and a geyser of steam shot onto that pretty French-looking light post, followed by some especially choice utterances.

I'm fairly sure Motley's lips turned up slightly as he and his dog ambled on down the street. Probably the dog got a real special treat later on, maybe even another pig's ear.

A Favorite Ploy

Getting older allows some of us with Irish minds to play tricks on the innumerable folks making phone sale pitches. One of my favorite ploys is to pretend I'm hard of hearing, or that I have trouble understanding English. Then, I kind of stroke the salesperson who is likely to be from some foreign country called Diddlysquat. Finally, I allow the salesperson to be rescued by turning them over to my wife, who is Mrs. Guaranteed No-Buy!

My last fun call was from our TV provider, Dish. I fumbled around awhile, grasping for my mental straws, which is extremely easy for me to do! Then I pretended I thought she was selling me dishes. I stretched this absurdity right to the breaking point—making sure her dishes wouldn't break. Were they microwave-safe? How many are in a set? Part of my fun is just letting my mind go bananas! Then I sicced my tiger wife on her for the sure kill.

Sometimes I think the salespeople just play along. Perhaps they are bored. Wouldn't you be? Perhaps they have an ample dose of Polish-blonde genes—that's a double whammy! Anyhow, it is hard to imagine being that many quarts low! But then again, maybe the salespeople are pulling *my* leg, resulting in a triple whammy.

My good friend Dale Zumwalt had even more fun recently. He'd been receiving an irritating sales call at the same time every day. So, he poured a full glass of water to get ready. Then the solicitor called as expected and went into her spiel. My friend started pouring the water, raised up high, into the toilet. The saleslady said she knew what he was doing and it was very rude! He was delighted, especially when the sales calls stopped.

Salespeople take great pleasure in calling at mealtime. Last week we had a call from Quest. I could not resist and got right into my dumb act. This is done with a liberal sprinkling of, "Huh? And repeated utterances of, "What?" I finally responded that we would appreciate any bequest, as long as it was free.

My wife just received a humorous sales call. Joan has a subscription to a magazine called *Quick and Easy Crochet*. The sales lady repeatedly mispronounced crotchet, referring to the magazine as *Crotch-It*. Boy! I could have had fun with that saleslady! Do you suppose the salespeople from Diddlysquat country have a quick and easy crotch-it?

A while back, I entertained a call from a Mrs. Apple who thought I needed what she had. I told her in my halting English that I would take a bushel of Red Delicious and a small box of her crisp Granny Smiths. I did not need whatever she was selling, but I told her I would sure enjoy her big ripe "apples." One of my challenges is to see how long the Diddly-Squatters will stay on the phone.

My most recent phone query was on a touchy (often in the news) subject. The woman asked what I thought about same-sex marriages, and should marriage be confined to a man and woman? You know my resistance is extremely low. My response was, "No, it should be one man and three women." Click, over-and-out went the phone line.

I once non-adroitly turned the tables on myself while I was a student at Oregon State University. The phone rang and I sallied out, "Heaa Wooo, this is me. Is that you?" in my absolute dumbest phone voice. The caller said, "This is the Dean of Agriculture," and he asked to speak to Roger Ritchey. Well, I had to change my phone persona immediately, which of course was impossible and I felt like a complete idiot—which I happily am from time to time.

I hope God does not play a trick on me by rendering me deaf. Doggone, but it's fun to be retired! And perhaps a bit retarded as well.

The Eavesdropper

I awoke to the sounds of suitcase wheels thumping and rolling briskly on the concrete sidewalk, accompanied by the flip-flopping of shuffling sandals. This early morning sleep interruption was after some thoughtless ding-knob had allowed his car alarm to go off repeatedly during the night. My wife, Joan, oblivious to it all, blissfully played Rip Van Winkle, practicing for another Oscar nomination.

We were, most definitely, not sleeping in the bedroom of our quiet, country home. It was our ideal holiday getaway, and those intrusive noises were not supposed to happen. So, I decided to join the mix.

It was five a.m. and my mental alarm had been bonging repeatedly in my thick Irish skull. I showered leisurely, enjoying the soothing water sounds. And then I deliberately disengaged my mind to let it meander with first day of vacation musings. I have learned that it takes two, or even three days for all of me to realize a vacation is the game plan. This almost out-of-mind and out-of-body sensation is rather strange, but certainly a delightful transformation. I liken it to old, tired, and deprived nerve endings suddenly realizing they have something to live for.

Slowly and quietly I dressed so as not wake Van Winkle. No stupid sandals for me! I think a sandal's main accomplishment is to spread apart your big toes. Then you end up with a size wider width, plus burning athlete's foot between those other unhappy toes. I have occasionally wondered how many sandals get caught in escalators. Well, Congress could commission another study or... we could just count the mangled toes.

Going down the outside stairs, the first person I spot is a straighter-than-a-cue-stick U.S. Marine, all spiffy and, for sure, no sandals on this guy. It was a respectful, "Good morning, sir," to brighten my day. I had noticed a sizable gathering of proud military personnel the day before, as Joan and I strolled around the motel grounds.

I sauntered on down to the motel office. I don't walk fast anyways, so naturally I was just turtleing along in my holiday mindset. In contrast, the Latino gardeners were scurrying around like ants. I smiled at a couple of the workers as I strode by. Then I settled into a comfy chair between two huge palm plants with a cup of coffee and a newspaper to get my morning fix.

The military bunch checked out and, after their noisy exit, I enjoyed a few minutes of quiet. Then the night clerk, a grizzled, pear-shaped older gentleman, made a comment to his Latino helper. "Wow, they (the military) left owing over thirty-three thousand dollars. The last two army groups insisted on paying before they left."

He received a "What's new?" grunt from the Latino fellow.

The grizzled clerk continued his accounting. "That is twenty-two thousand dollars and change for room charges, and eleven thousand for the food, including the banquet bash."

The Latino guy just gave him a hard stare back, after glancing at me. I thought, *The Latino has more smarts than the clerk.*

Just then, the office door burst open and a chic woman in her mid-thirties flashed up to the desk. I guessed she was huffing and puffing from her super-mad dash to the office. This babe is a regular, I gathered, by the desk clerk's familiarity. Then she dropped some papers on the floor and said, "Shit." The clerk handed her a room receipt and she tore back out the door. That left me thinking that her torrid life did not have western world stress, and that it was a good thing she didn't arrive at the office during the military mess. But then, last night's military party might have been the reason she was running late.

Then I said to myself, *I sure don't need this newspaper for my entertainment.* Because....

Next, the Incredible Hulk entered, in overdrive, powering his way into the office. A big, tall, muscular dude with the sleeves of his sweatshirt chopped off to show his bulging biceps. Sunglasses were perched on top of his noggin as if he was halfway to Hollywood. His chest looked like the front end of a Sherman tank and he dramatically flexed his biceps, which were larger than a fat person's thigh. His arm arteries throbbed like the throat of a Louisiana bullfrog, perceptible through the layers of tattoos. The top of his head was shaved and polished to a high sheen—shinier than all the jewelry hanging from every visible appendage. The only thing out of sync was his high-pitched voice. So high, he ought to think about an operation, or maybe he'd already been under the knife too many times. I choose not to make eye contact. But I did give him a huge plus for not wearing sandals.

The San Diego circus show continued!

But this time it was a surprise. A normal-looking couple—probably in their fifties—strode up to the desk. Well, the woman did the striding and her puppy dog spouser ambled along like someone wishing he wasn't there.

The gutsy woman stated firmly, "We need to change our room." She proceeded to tackle the tough negotiating. Her trained puppy husband made himself busy looking at the travel brochures and the floor covering. I was thinking, *That man has had practice doing that.*

It turns out the couple's daughter was being married at the facility the next day and according to the woman, the daughter needed to secure a room with a bay view. "Yes," the woman stated, "I will reluctantly pay for a one-hundred-dollar per night upgrade." Finally, after all the hard talking was done, hubby tried to placate the word-battered night clerk.

Then the day clerk arrived—a young woman long on looks and short on brains, judging by her chirpy good mornings as she settled in for the sunny day's fun. I fully comprehended why old Grizz, the night clerk, was chosen for the night owl shift. He was definitely not going to be accused of Hanky or Panky!

Thankfully, Joan arrived just then to save me from falling into some southern California lair, and we checked out of the San Diego Zoo.

In closing, but still on the topic of travel, I must relate a scene that occurred on our Holland America cruise one day at lunchtime. There were only four African-American couples on board the *Stadendam*. One black couple seemed not at all inclined to mingle. But a four-times-divorced lady (she was boasting) cornered the reclusive black couple near the football field-long buffet bar. This ex, ex, ex, ex woman was a loud, non-stop talker carrying on about her second husband. The volume of her voice just kept rising as she progressed into what was obviously a pet subject. She described hubby number two as—"So self-centered, he was convinced he looked good without his false teeth!"

And I realized this is precisely the reason some single or divorced people take cruises. They've already worn out everybody for miles around their home with their gassing.

The woman's avalanche of talking continued for quite a while and finally the black guy, squeezing a word in, asked her, "Why did you marry him?"

She tilted her head back and roared, "For his money! For once in my life, I wanted to be rich and I was, for a little while."

Likeable Chores ... Again & Again

The flames seem hungry this morning
Feeding or starting my fire is different every day
Some fires are weak and feeble
Some roar like a chimney fire
Like people, all are different
I guess that is one of my loves
The differences and the sameness
Both together

With luck, snapping, cracking and popping
Talking to me
We have this intimate conversation
The small flame growing
To a blaze
Throwing heat into our space
Heating my fingers, my bones, my core
The old girl dog blinking her appreciation
Another piece of starter wood
Alder, cedar or madrone

The dog nudges me
It's my turn now
Out the door we go
I hear the distant ocean boom
The tide is coming in

The birds, seeing us, chirp their approval
Except the squawking jays

I'm always too late for them
I place some millet & check the suet
Fetch the paper to sate my news deficit
Must see what Pickles (me) &
Blondie (Joan) are doing

Add another piece of wood
Oak or maple for the longer burn
I put my back to the stove and gather warmth
I'll get my oatmeal and yogurt now
Along with another cup of tea
And welcome the day
Again and again

Hugging Seventy?

Hugging our seventies
We now know
How fast
Time slips away

Our Sixties tore by
Now just a blip
In the rearview mirror
So grab all
The hugs you can

Seventy,
Like many things
Happens only once
But luckily we can
Keep right on
Chugging and hugging

So bust your butt
Because…
Life truly Depends
On Huggies!

SECTION 2

Three To A Hill:
a tribute to my uncle
Dwight L. McCue

Three To A Hill

This story is about my uncle, Dwight Lytton McCue, a man whose life story just had to be told.

If you're wondering where the title of this story came from, it's because Uncle Dwight planted his sweet corn in hills—three seeds to each one. That was a practice common up to the early 1900s, and probably still used in many places through the 1950s. Planting corn in hills may have been a holdover from the Native Americans, who placed a whole fish along with their seeds in each hole, the fish serving as slow-release fertilizer. Dwight held with that custom as well, and if the corn all sprouted, and if the crows or coons did not get it, well, all was "swell." (Uncle Dwight often used the word "swell.") He'd say the corn was growing "three to a hill," a good start towards making a crop.

But I'm getting way ahead of myself.

Dwight was my mother's older brother and he was my favorite uncle. I had a total of eight uncles, but three of those relations remained in Minnesota, so the distance eliminated them from my young life.

Uncle Dwight was just three years older than my mom,

and the two of them were bonded—almost joined at the hip. Dwight watched out for Mom like a fierce bird predator when they were young, but his vigilance diminished as my older sister and I gradually assumed some of his hawkish role. However, later in life, Dwight occasionally reasserted his big bird role.

Dwight and Mom were the last two children of the four born to my grandparents, Wilbur Birdsong (aka Buchanan) McCue and Margaret Ellen (Nichols) McCue. Dwight was born on November 25, 1903 in St. Paul, Minnesota, and he almost made it into the next century, dying on June 7, 1999, in Forest Grove, Oregon.

Straight out of the chute, Dwight L. McCue was a highly complex person with enormous capabilities. The veneer personality he presented to the world six days a week was that of a middle-of-the-road conservative individual. But by high school, his natural superiority was evident.

UNCLE'S FETCHING UP

Dwight Lytton, or D.L. as some people called him, was named after D.L. Moody, a well-known fire-and-hell preacher to whom his mother was particularly partial. Grandma Margaret Ellen hailed from iron-willed religious people of Nortonville, Kansas. According to Uncle Dwight, his father, my Grandpa, was not raised by his real father.

As a young man, Grandpa Mac had left his home near the Wabash River in Indiana, and went to work for Grandma's parents on their Kansas farm.

My mom (Margaret Helen McCue Ritchey) often referred to Dwight as D.L., but most everyone else just called him Dwight. Dwight usually called my mother "Sister."

Their three older brothers were Orral, Wiloughby (Wilby), and Merritt. The eldest, Orral, was Grandpa's son from an earlier relationship, but all four boys grew up close. The boys—and of course Mom, too—were clean, orderly, hardworking, religious, and honest. There was no other way, given their parental influences.

Wilby's nickname was "Shorty" because that's what he was. Wilby was five inches shorter than Merritt, the tallest brother. Orral was next in height, and then Dwight.

A characteristic common to the McCue family was the twinkle in their eyes. I think Wilby's eyes had the most pronounced shine, but Dwight and Merritt were close contenders. Dwight had a warm, two-handed grasp whenever he shook a person's hand, which convincingly conveyed he was glad to meet them or to see them again. Wilby and Merritt were also very hands-on and would get close enough so we could feel their breath.

The four boys tended to be labeled as "characters" and luckily, I saw this facet of their personalities from time to time. Acting out, or carrying on with each other, was most prevalent in Wilby and Merritt, but I was not around the oldest brother, Orral, very much, so he could have been the same way. All five siblings had a keen sense of humor.

Orral pointing and Merritt on the ladder at Dwight's, 1955

Orral standing on porch, Grandpa Mac McCue, Wilby, and Grandma
on top step, Merritt, Dwight, and my mom, Helen below, 1912

Grandpa Mac loved to watch and listen to summer thunderstorms, so he'd sit on his Minnesota front porch in his wooden chair (which has been handed down to me) for a front row seat to those incredibly black skies with white or yellow lightning zigzagging like crazy.

Swearing or cussing was limited in the McCue family, most likely because of Grandma's influence. My mom occasionally used the term "slop-ass" when referring to folks she didn't much respect, but those who fell even further in her estimation became a "shit-ass."

Dwight on donkey, 1912
(Note: It was the Year of the Ass on the Chinese calendar)

Neither Uncle Dwight nor Mom smoked and practically never drank, whereas the three older siblings did smoke, and so did Grandpa, mainly using pipes filled with Prince Albert tobacco when he was inside the house. I found a number of White Owl cigar boxes, and learned that Grandpa would puff on, or at least chew the ends of, these pungent-smelling long-lasting smokes while outdoors. Those neat little cigar boxes are handy for storing lots of whatevers.

Nicotine, and the resulting stomach cancer, finally got to Grandpa at the age of eighty-four. And cancer of the lung claimed the middle brother, Merritt. Uncle Wilby rolled his own cigarettes with Bull Durham tobacco and for whatever reason, he tended to smoke less than his brothers did. It took Wilby so darn long to roll a smoke that he probably inhaled less. First, he was careful not to spill the tobacco out of the small cloth pouch, and then he would methodically lick the paper so it would stay rolled. I rather enjoyed watching Wilby go through that aromatic routine partially because he got such a kick out it and because he liked me watching him. He always had a glimmer of a smile when a roll-your-own smoke event was taking place.

Wilby died from emphysema, but the doctors tended to believe the cause was as much from train coal dust as from tobacco. But now, thinking about it some, rolling his own smoke doesn't quite compute with Wilby's passion for riding an old Indian motorcycle and winning all the County Fair races. Or, well, maybe it does. One thing I noticed about the smallest of my uncles was that he was quicker than a cat, even way into his eighties.

Surprisingly, none of the five siblings had a problem with alcohol even though Grandpa liked a cool one or two on a hot summer day. Actually, Grandpa was known to get drunk now and then as a young man, something that— sadly—I managed to do myself in my youthful days.

Wiloughby "Wilby" McCue, 1985

I find it interesting, and rather humorous, how Grandma "cured" her youngest two children—Mom and Dwight—from imbibing in suds. She accomplished this by emphatically stating that the horse pee they saw as youngsters in the St. Paul streets was the beginnings of frothy, foamy beer. The lesson set like concrete. Grandma had saved them from—according to her—a mortal sin. Looking back now, my life would have gone better without the alcohol I consumed. It is a good thing our kidneys and liver can't talk, but when they do, it is generally time to get ready to say goodbye.

Grandma detested smoking as well as getting tipsy, and when Grandpa died, she built a hot bonfire, burning all Grandpa's pipes, leather pouches, and leftover tobacco. At least that's what Dwight told me.

Well, I am with Grandma on this smoking matter because I vividly recall being at my grandfather's deathbed with my dad where Grandpa was propped up. Cancer had spread to his bones, which was excruciatingly painful. Painkillers weren't nearly as effective back in the 1950s, so this tough old guy, with tears rolling down his cheeks, told us he couldn't wait until the cancer spread to his heart. And when I say tough, that is exactly what he was. For example, Grandpa Mac McCue fell off his two-story roof while doing repairs when he was eighty-something years old. He broke a leg, but that hardly slowed him down.

Dwight's childhood was spent in several towns in Minnesota, including New Ulm, which had been settled predominately by German families. The McCues lived in New Ulm during World War I. Back then, the war was known as The Great War and The War to End All Wars. We have sure managed to mess up that pronouncement.

Two of the older McCue brothers served in the U.S. Military during World War II. Wilby was a Marine, and Merritt was in the Navy. A family story trickled down through the years about the time another sailor stole Merritt's pants off the wash line, so he grabbed someone else's. But Merritt was caught and reprimanded. There was some bad fallout with him having to cross "The Big Pond," which is how they referred to the Atlantic Ocean.

I find it interesting that several New Ulm German words rubbed off on the McCue clan and ever after, certain German phrases snuck into their everyday talk such as "gutten morgen" (good morning), "zimmer" (room), and "gute nacht" (good night). Sometimes Dwight and Mom would launch into a little *sprechen sie deutsche* when I was a kid, and they'd be smiling all the while.

Losing one's temper was a McCue family activity. The entire McCue clan—except for Grandma—had visible and highly audible tempers, and that tendency came direct from Grandpa Mac. Grandma would just clam up when she was upset.

Dwight and Merritt in front of their home at 317 S. State Street, New Ulm, Minnesota, 1917

Uncle Dwight had the worst temper of the siblings, and Mom was next. Both of them could sure light 'em up and lay into whoever was around. I found it best to walk out of the room whenever they got going, a trick I learned from

Dad. Folks generally don't holler very long without an audience, and shouting at a wall isn't much fun. Uncle Dwight never got mad at me. But now Mom... well, she was a *serious* matter and truth be told, she generally correctly had me pegged as the culprit.

Dwight is the boy leaning over his father's shoulder. Photo taken in Mac McCue's office at Eagle Rolling Mills, New Ulm, around 1912

My Grandpa Mac McCue was the head electrical engineer for Eagle Rolling Mill in New Ulm, and had 75 men working under him making flour. Grandpa was also instrumental in organizing a large U.S. victory parade after World War I because he was very patriotic. The parade would include several tanks and big howitzers guns, plus assorted other military equipment. That event eventually became part of Armistice Day celebrations.

My wife, Joan, and I traveled to New Ulm, Germany, in 1989 when our son, Dale Cline, was in the Air Force. And we were lucky enough to visit that other, newer New Ulm in Minnesota in 1995.

1917 Victory Day Parade tank

One of Dwight's favorite jobs as a youngster was in a candy factory. He said he would arrive back home in the evening with candy stuck to the soles of his shoes, and beguile me with tales of how much he managed to eat while at work. He loved candy until he died, and would purchase Van Dyne's or See's chocolates on a regular basis.

Dwight also worked at a telegraph office that required him to type on a machine with an extra-long carriage. He said that typewriter was quite the challenge for him for the first few days. But typing became his preferred way to communicate for the rest of his life. He could type 90 words per minute, but Mom had him beat because she could hit 120 words per minute. They both whizzed along on the old manual keyboards.

Orral and Wilby started working for the Minnesota Railroad Lines railroad and both were awarded lifetime passes at retirement.

Dwight spent a year or so assisting Merritt, who had a job installing electrical plants throughout the Midwest. Merritt, by the way, was called "Slip" by the family. Dwight and Merritt were exceptionally close because they had similar personalities and because those two were most like their father. Dwight and Merritt called me "Kiddo," although they occasionally used this moniker for other boys too.

My Uncle Dwight had an independent gene or two—something that seems to run in our family. Perhaps it's just the Irish coming out, but somewhere along the line, Dwight hatched the idea of going to Oregon and raising laying hens. He told me that Merritt had said, 'You're crazy, Dwight, it won't work and you'll soon be back in Minnesota with your tail between your legs.'

When Dwight wasn't dissuaded, Merritt added, 'You're not from the country and you don't siccum about raising chickens or about farming.' (*Don't know siccum* referred to people who couldn't cut the mustard.) I got the strong impression that "Slip" wanted Dwight to stick around as his sidekick in the expanding electrical business.

Dwight with Dad's Buick in 1923

207

But Grandpa and Grandma took Dwight along when they traveled to Oregon on vacation in 1926 in a brand new Buick. Grandpa Mac was a Buick man and that 1926 was his fourth. His first car had been a 1916 four-cylinder. His second was a 1919 six-cylinder Buick. Both were open-top cars—convertibles!

Dwight complained about the lack of signs and poor roads, and about following the Yellowstone "trail" through Montana and Wyoming. Sometimes they just drove by the seat of their pants, or they followed the sunshine. Dwight said Grandpa Mac had a real good sense of direction. It turns out my mom and I inherited this knack too.

It makes sense that Dwight's chicken business idea was "hatched" during that western adventure because many Oregon chicken plans were "laid" in Minnesota during the following winter. Dwight had connected with people who had a keen eye for the purchase of suitable acreage, and others from whom he could get a contract loan.

He also developed a plan for finding a wife willing to put her neck on the line in support of his dream. The lucky woman turned out to be Eva Newton, a gal he met in St. Paul who agreed to work right along with her "honey," as she called Dwight. When Uncle Dwight took up with Eva, he left behind a few broken-hearted gals. I know this morsel because my mom's best friend, Lucy Windland, was one of them. Mom and Lucy kept in contact all of their lives, and I was fortunate enough to meet Lucy once during a trip to Minnesota. Interestingly, Dwight always read Lucy's letters written to Mom and Lucy wanted to be kept abreast of Dwight's doings.

Obviously, Dwight was a planner deluxe and he *did* make it out to Oregon, and he did start a chicken farm.

Uncle Dwight emphatically conveyed to me that most "sane" people know enough to escape the dreadful 40-degrees-below-zero Minnesota winters and its hot, humid summers. So, after Grandpa and Grandma retired, they moved to Oregon and built a nice two-story country home with a full basement less than 100 yards southeast of Dwight's farmstead. That house was situated just across the Oregon Electric tracks at the north end of Maple Street in Forest Grove.

Dwight L. McCue, shortly before leaving for Oregon in 1927,
at Cumo Park, Minnesota

Margaret Helen McCue Ritchey and Dwight McCue in Oregon, 1928
Isn't this a priceless photo?

Dwight L. McCue at his wedding, 1929
You can understand why Uncle Dwight had girlfriends

A DOG PERSON

Dwight, like many in our family, was always a dog person. The family had a dog named Shep, and Dwight said that as a little boy, he and Shep would head down to a cow pasture and fall asleep with the cows grazing right next to them. The family's next dog was a smaller black and white named Gippie, who was also a family favorite.

When Dwight started his layer operation in Oregon, his first dog was a German shepherd named Pal. They were devoted to each other. Pal was purchased by Grandpa McCue in Minnesota and shipped by rail to Forest Grove.

The next dog, also a German shepherd, was named Lucky, and he was right in his prime when an unfortunate incident occurred. My sister was giving him snacks, but somehow the dog ended up biting her scalp. It was not a serious injury, but Dwight chose to get rid of that dog. He never would tell me what he did with Lucky. He'd just look back at me with a blank stare and that made me assume the worst. Lucky, who wasn't, was the last of that excellent shepherd breed for Uncle Dwight.

A number of years later, Dwight brought home a smaller dog that weighed maybe twenty-five or thirty pounds. And daggone... there was another bad, sad deal. Dwight was mowing a pasture with a six-foot sickle mower mounted on his John Deere tractor. The little dog got in front of the sickle-bar and Uncle mowed his back leg off.

Dwight rushed her to Dr. Elwin Coon, the local veterinarian, and he saved the dog's life. It got along well on three legs for several years, except his cat-chasing days were over.

Dwight chose not to have another dog in the latter part of his life. I asked him why, but he never gave me a good answer. I thought a critter would have helped him with his later loneliness.

Pal and Dwight, 1929

EXACTNESS IN DRAWINGS

I believe most folks are lucky to be exceptional in one endeavor, but Dwight L. McCue was at the top of the heap in several. It's a toss-up to know which of his talents to talk about first, so I'll start with his drawing skills because they surfaced first. Dwight's artistic ability was probably the least known of his talents because he did the intricate mechanical drawings early in life, before his 1927 migration to Oregon.

Dwight took drawing classes to learn how to create intricate drawings in the early 1920s. I have nearly a hundred of those drawings and they are impressive in their detail. This attention to detail was a facet of his personality for the remainder of Dwight's life. He wanted everything to be very clean and concise. For sure, he was not a slop-ass.

I never tire of studying these mechanical drawings because of their incredible detail. I keep a few posted in my shop, just to inspire me. Today, of course, these kinds of illustrations are generated by computer programs rather than by the human hand. But that kinda seems like cheating.

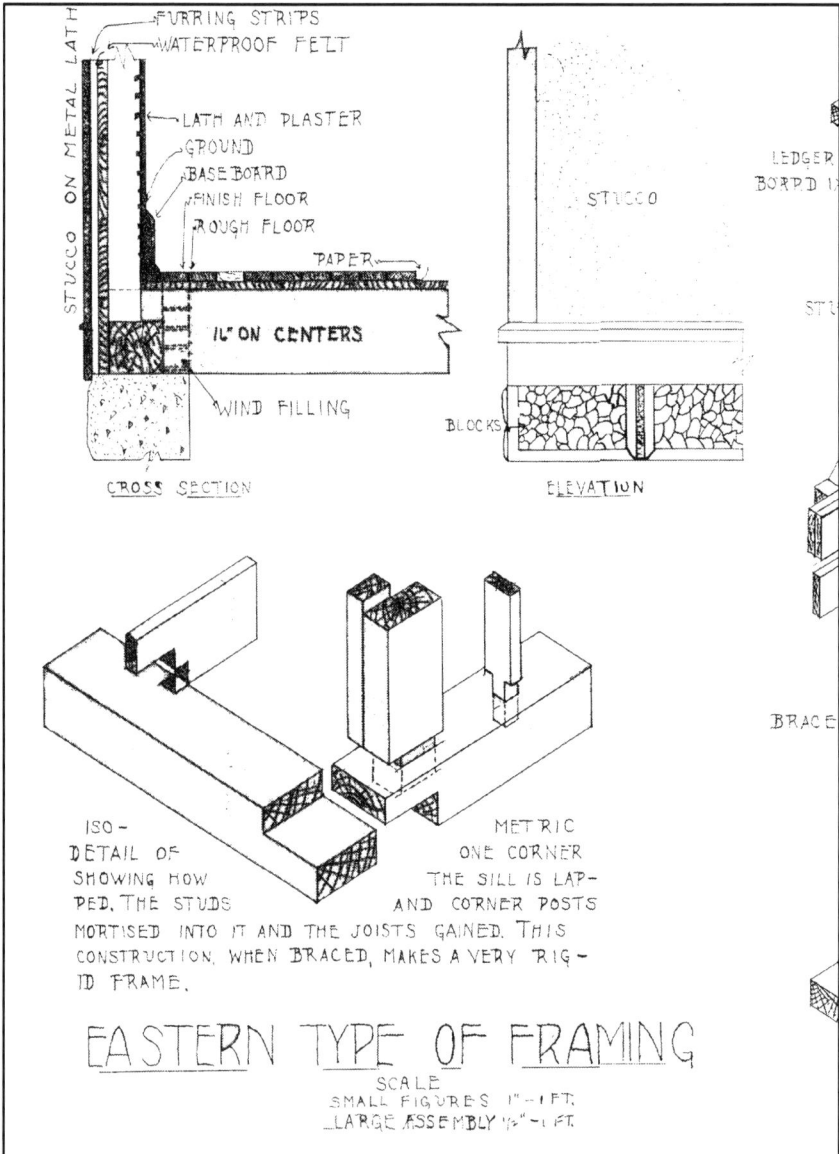

FURRING STRIPS
WATERPROOF FELT
LATH AND PLASTER
GROUND
BASEBOARD
FINISH FLOOR
ROUGH FLOOR
PAPER
STUCCO ON METAL LATH
16" ON CENTERS
WIND FILLING

CROSS SECTION

STUCCO
LEDGER BOARD
STU
BLOCKS

ELEVATION

BRACE

ISO-
DETAIL OF
SHOWING HOW
PED, THE STUDS

METRIC
ONE CORNER
THE SILL IS LAP-
AND CORNER POSTS

MORTISED INTO IT AND THE JOISTS GAINED. THIS
CONSTRUCTION, WHEN BRACED, MAKES A VERY RIG-
ID FRAME.

EASTERN TYPE OF FRAMING

SCALE
SMALL FIGURES 1"=1 FT.
LARGE ASSEMBLY ½"=1 FT.

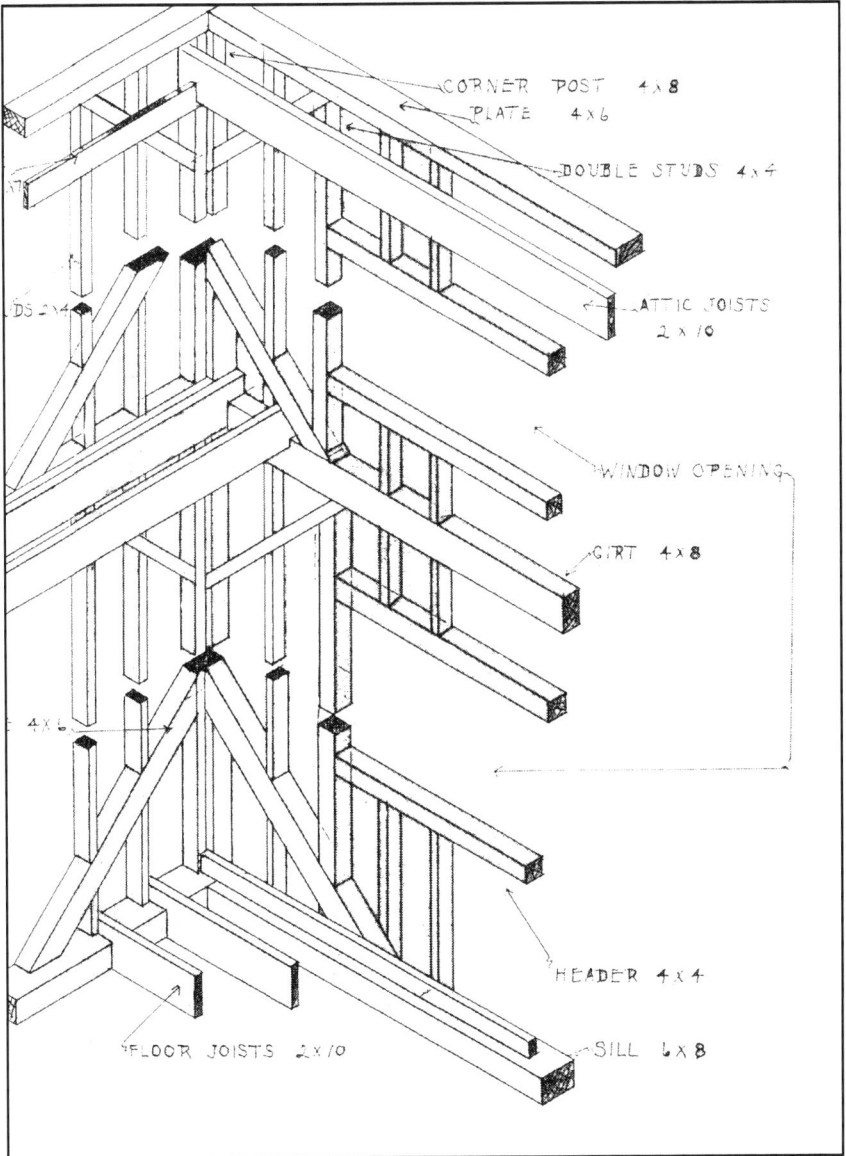

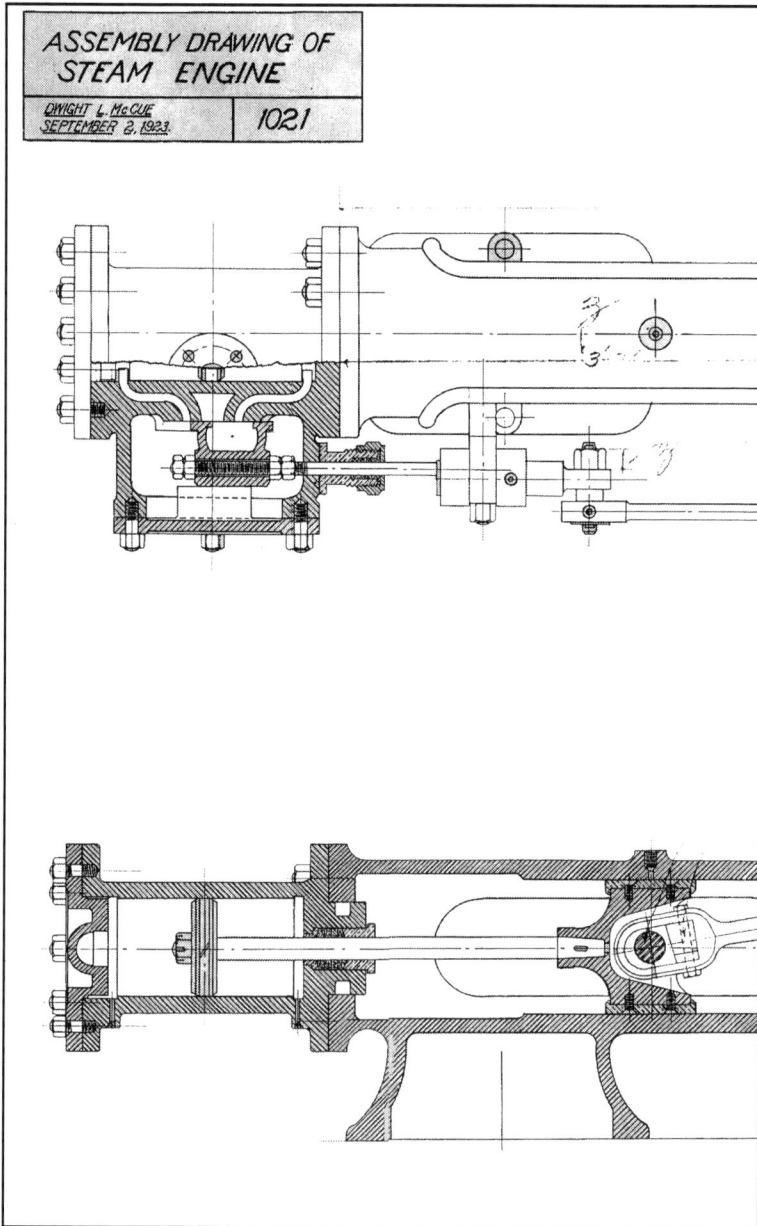

ASSEMBLY DRAWING OF
STEAM ENGINE

DWIGHT L. McCUE
SEPTEMBER 2, 1923.   1021

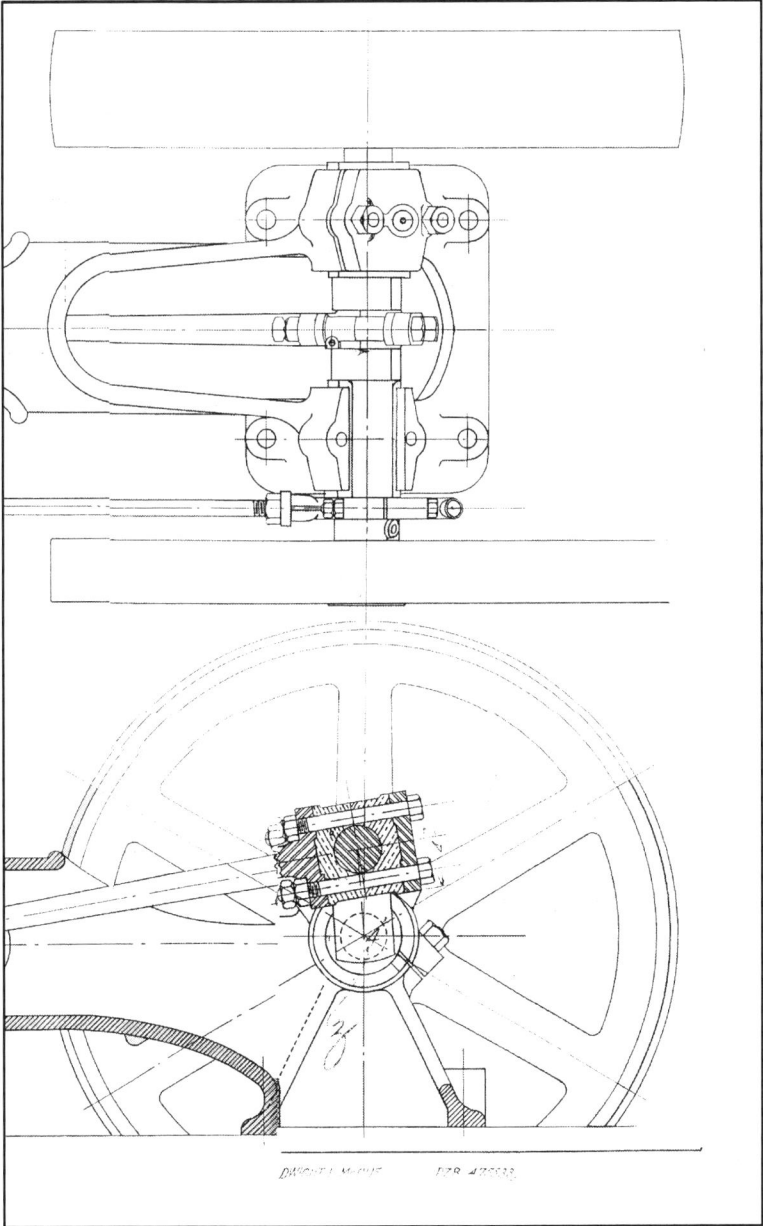

BUILDING FARM STRUCTURES

Uncle Dwight's second skill was as a carpenter and woodworker. Dwight built all three of the large chicken-laying houses on his farm property, and I would guess their dimensions to be 40 feet wide by 120 feet long, divided into sections. All these chicken-laying buildings were oriented to the east and west, with south-facing windows that opened to vent hot air during the summer. The north side of each section was used as an enclosed roosting area, and windows for cross ventilation. Box nests were attached to the walls on the east and west sides of each section, and the eggs were gathered two or three times per day. The feed, grain, grit, and ground up oyster shells were stored on the west ends, in an outside metal feed storage bin that could hold several tons. Dwight had obtained the plans for these well-designed structures from Oregon State University.

The cleaning of the roosts twice a year was accomplished by opening narrow slots on the north side and then pushing the manure from under the roosts with long-handled scrapers. It was my "privilege" to help with this cleaning a time or two, which would uncork the smell of ammonia—and *whooee!* Chickens have a lockdown on that distinctive biting odor. The waste of no other farm animal smells as offensively sharp of ammonia, and I do know of what I speak.

I've managed to hold onto one of those wide scrapers, a metal scoop shovel, two of Dwight's small feed scoops and several of the many wood-framed windows that were held in place with old-fashioned putty. I bribed a skilled artist to paint farm scenes on a few of those old windows, and the paintings of old barns still grab a few oohs and aahs in appreciation.

Dwight building chicken house at age 24, 1928

Brother Wilby McCue helping to build chicken house, 1928

Dwight with his white Leghorn chickens, 1930

The photo above shows Grandpa Mac feeding the chickens wheat kernels on the ground just south of their "A" chicken house. The B house was adjacent to this one, and the C house was behind Grandpa's home. Notice the M shape he created as he scattered the grain. That was deliberate. I do not know whose grand idea it was, nor what was behind the practice, but I did something similar at Oregon State University when I was a junior in 1962 and serving as president of the Agriculture Council. Maybe this kind of stuff seeps out of our genes. At Oregon State University, I did it to display graphically with people (not chickens) how the Agricultural Council functioned. Our member's layout resembled a wagon wheel with spokes. A photo was taken by someone standing on an elevated stairway. I had not seen this chicken M at the time.

Dwight also built numerous brooder houses on skids for young chickens or pullets raised in a large fenced area during the late spring and summer. Decades later, I used these six-by-eight foot specially designed brooder houses for bottle-feeding small calves I was raising to sell.

In the story, "The Good, The Bad, and The Ugly" included in my first book, *Hankering For The Way It Was,* I wrote about a large pack of homeless starving dogs that were killing Dwight's pullets, and what we had to do to end that carnage. Those pullets had been housed in these brooder or "range" houses.

Once the laying houses were finished, Uncle Dwight built a small loft barn for a milk cow and a steer or two. I often helped him put hay in the barn, and occasionally would milk their old bossy cow when Dwight had to be away too many hours. On the Sundays when I helped with putting his hay or straw bales in the barn, we'd eat lunch in Grandpa Mac's home. By then, Grandpa had passed away, but Toby Morton, the housekeeper, still lived there and we'd eat lunch in the kitchen nook. Toby had been hired to help take care of Grandpa and Grandma in their latter years. The cozy kitchen nook had east and south-facing windows. I remember Grandma's ancient, brightly colored milk pitcher. It had (and has) a small chip on the pour lip.

Toby was a real good worker, and had a son one year older than me. The son, Norm, and I never got along for several reasons—some my fault and some his, as our egos were in constant battle. Uncle Dwight became that boy's surrogate dad too.

Uncle Dwight completely remodeled his original one-and-a-half-story farmhouse into a single-story with a huge fireplace. There was a small office just off the kitchen, and the huge woodstove in there heated his entire house. I would often sit and talk with him in that room and I swear it was always 80 degrees Fahrenheit in there during the winter. Even then, Dwight would be wearing a sweater. It was his practice to start the fire in October, and because he could clean the stove without letting the fire die out, the same fire would still be going in April. When the weather warmed and it was time to let the fire go out, he would say, "Bye, fire." Now, sometimes I whisper those words, too.

WOODWORKING TALENTS

Dwight really enjoyed his Shop-Smith wood lathe, which meant my uncle generally smelled like chicken feed and sawdust. The odor of chicken feed can dominate a room, but it isn't particularly offensive, at least to me, having been raised on a farm with chickens, turkeys, hogs, and cows. We even had a few old horses to pull things when I was a kid.

W.B. McCue and Dwight's dog, Pal, Forest Grove, 1932

All of the precision-made cabinets inside Uncle Dwight's house were constructed by him, plus he was always making something for somebody who didn't have his woodworking capabilities.

Dwight had to clear quite a sizeable area on his eventual 85 acres. The stand was predominately oak and fir, with their large, deep root systems. So Uncle Dwight became adept at using dynamite for stump blowing and was still buying sticks, caps, and fuses into the 1980s. Dynamite was packed in sawdust to cushion it, and I thought it had an unusual odor, not offensive, just distinctive. Dwight told me it was necessary to go as far south as Newberg for the best box price. I think he rather enjoyed having the 4th of July several times a year. Two acres of trees and brush remained standing when he died. He had been saving those trees for his future firewood supply. Of course, Uncle Dwight cut and split all the wood for his two woodstoves, the big one in his house and a smaller unit in his garage-shop. A lot of happy birds and critters made their home in those remaining acres.

I think most of our family, me included, tend toward being pyromaniacs—we sure love building and tending bonfires, and burning up roots and leaves.

A rather odd article of Uncle Dwight's that I've hung onto would not interest most people—Dwight's old chopping block. I do not know what type of wood it is, or how old, but this block has darn sure got the right heft, with numerous old saw and wedge marks. It still gets a lot of hard use every year, so it's been seasoned by his sweat and now mine. Well, I don't have a favorite war horse to bury with me, and I'm sure if I had one, I still wouldn't, but I've been thinking about that old chopping block....

RECORD KEEPING AND EGG PROFITS

I saw Uncle Dwight's records for the egg laying operation many times. Once I even led an agriculture class from Forest Grove High School out to his farm to view and learn from his methods. There were numerous categories such as "eggs-laid-per-hen," which, as I recall, exceeded 300 eggs produced per year by each of his White Leghorn chickens, the heaviest layers in those days.

Dwight also sold hatching eggs for a very good price and he told me that his record of production statistics helped justify the high price he charged. His precise records calculated the cost of producing a dozen eggs down to one-tenth-of-a-cent. So, he was happy, the roosters were happy, and those hens kept a'laying.

Uncle Dwight also kept meticulous records on how each field produced, what was planted and when, plus details about the fertilizers or any sprays used. His records went back more than 40 years and all the data illustrates how precisely his numerals or printed notations were kept.

I marveled at this ability because he obviously immensely enjoyed the demands of mental exactness.

Uncle Dwight separated one henhouse into two sections for his hatching-egg production. One time, a couple of rosters got into the adjacent pen and fertilized some of those eggs. A small red blood spot shows up in the yolk when that happens, so our family had to help him eat those eggs. We'd clean each egg then candle them, which shows the blood spot. Candling an egg is done by placing the egg in front of a lit light bulb.

Dwight supplied all of the eggs direct to the Forest Grove School system and thereby eliminated the middleman. At one point, he was shipping eggs as far east as New York City. Hard to believe, but it's true. I wonder if those Easterners got any of those rooster-fertilized bloodspot eggs.

Dwight never changed his chickens to Daylight Savings Time because chickens especially become upset when their timing is disturbed. So he and the layers stayed with an established schedule. Most dairymen I knew remained on standard time, too.

Dwight and my dad, R. Glenn Ritchey, were both prodigious and precise record keepers regarding every aspect affecting farm profits. It was my privilege to absorb, and hopefully learn, a few tips from them. I wish I had a copy of Dwight's egg-producing records because his detailed accounting was as good as what can be obtained using today's computers, but he was fifty years ahead of his time.

And Uncle Dwight sure knew how to maximize profits. One example was selling his eggs and excess raspberries, apples, or whatever—from a farm honor-system stand. Naturally, they knew all the long-winded talkers who drove up to get eggs and produce, so when they showed up, Dwight would duck out a back door of the egg-cleaning room. Dwight had way too much to do to stand around jawing.

Another example of profitable business acumen was when Dwight and Eva developed a small subdivision near where my grandparent's home was located on the original 85 acres. It is now platted as the McCue Subdivision, which kinda has a Scotch-Irish ring to it. That land ended up with thirty lots, including a couple of cul-de-sacs where several acres of filberts had once grown and Uncle's chickens had happily clucked.

QUALITY WHEELS

When Uncle Dwight found something good, he stayed with it, and took excellent care of everything he owned. That habit was drummed into me, too, at a very early age— *If it's good enough to buy, it's worth maintaining.* Both sides of my family—the McCues and the Ritcheys—lived by that rule. Especially in regards to their automobiles. The family's first car was a 1916 open-topped Buick. Once they had a car, the garage was where it was sheltered and protected. The car's tires were even pulled off, wrapped in newspaper, and stored in the basement during their Minnesota winters. Grandpa Mac happily drove Buicks for most of his life. Dwight, too, was a Buick man.

Dwight also had several John Deere tractors and always had one of their riding lawn mowers on hand. His pickup truck was a 1949 Chevrolet flatbed. This raised flatbed had removable side racks because that was handy for unloading one hundred pound sacks of feed or egg crates holding twelve dozen eggs. That pickup made weekly trips to Portland. I went along a time or two and I remember how much fun it was coming up Canyon Road with a full load of feed, that six-cylinder engine just humming. Equipment made right after World War II was pretty good stuff or *skookum*—a word Dwight used to indicate quality stuff. The only products I recall as being inferior in those times were the first Japanese nails that made it to our farm stores. Some of those nails weren't much better than a wet noodle, but eventually their imports improved in quality. Dwight kept that Chevy flatbed truck into the 1990s, at which point he sold it to his good friend, Lester Heisler. Unbelievably, the truck still had its original battery and tires.

MUSICAL TALENT

Dwight taught himself to play the drums and he put together a band with friends from Forest Grove. Stella (Melville) Stahl "plunked away" on the piano. Simon "Si" Isenstein reportedly couldn't read a note of music, but played a fine fiddle by ear. There may have been five band members total, but I don't have the names of the others.

Si Isenstein owned a nice furniture store and was the father of Brenda, a pretty girl in my high school class with a swell personality. Sadly, Brenda died from breast cancer before the age of sixty.

According to Harold Johnson, now 96 years old, he saw the "Do-Se-Dos" play in Forest Grove many times and noted that Si would get more animated and lively as the night sped along. The Do-Se-Dos band played regularly at local dances in both Washington and Yamhill counties.

When he wasn't up on stage performing, Dwight was out on the dance floor. He loved to dance. And women liked to dance with him because he was slick and smooth on his feet, plus good with small talk.

Maybe Dwight got his musical talent from his father, Mac McCue. Back in Minnesota, when Grandpa was a young man, he'd sung in a quartet, but once he moved to Oregon and lived near our family, he would often sing old-time songs to my sister, Carol, and me. One he especially liked was "Old Dan Tucker."

Carol and I learned the song "Buttons and Bows," which we sang to Grandpa a couple of times and that sure made him smile.

Many years later, after Uncle Dwight quit playing the drums, he sold them to John McCoy, another young neighborhood boy who Dwight befriended and to whom he served as a surrogate father. Like mine, Johnny's father had died at a very young age, the very same year my dad had passed away. Johnny ended up working for Stimson Lumber for 49 years, helping to keep everything running shipshape. Working for one outfit your whole life was common back in those days, and maybe both employers and employees were happier for it. At least two of my high school classmates, Kenny Hedin and Bill Holscher, spent all their "9-to-5" days at Tektronix, Inc. in Beaverton.

Dwight told me that he'd always wanted to have children, but that a doctor told him he was just shooting "blanks." I like to think it was God's plan for him, because of the several boys he nurtured, including me, after my own dad died.

Grandpa Mac and my father died within a week of each other in 1950 and Mom was devastated. She was so shocked, she stayed flat in bed for more than two weeks. Her father and her husband were two of the three anchors in her life—Dwight being the third. At that point, Dwight was drawn back into our lives and once again he became his sister's protector and leaning post, as well as my stepfather.

I remember wondering—but just to myself—if Mom would ever get up. I also remember having a big knot in my stomach and noticing that my ten-year-old brain had emptied of all rational thought. It was like living in an empty void.

That was a horrible period in our lives. But one person sticks out—my Aunt Bert. She came over with food every day for us kids, and brought soup for Mom. I could hear their muted voices in the spare bedroom. For a long, long time, Mom refused to sleep in the bedroom she and Dad had shared, but finally she decided that the so-called "living" have to pick up and go on.

I guess Mom, my sister, and I eventually got tougher, but back then I built a wall around myself, which didn't work especially well. In fact, the walls compounded and extended my misery. The main point was that our little family of three—singularly and jointly—made it through the mourning period. Eventually, I learned to put on the right face, but most neighbor folks, and even family members, did not know what was going on in my gut. However, Dwight became a very steady mental, physical, and emotional presence in our lives.

DWIGHT'S FUN SIDE

My Uncle Dwight was great to just hang around with. One particular Sunday road trip to Astoria with Dwight and Toby (this was after Eva's death) was a hoot. Joan and my mother were, of course, along for the all-day jaunt. We drove the back roads to Vernonia, and from there northwest into the boonies, arriving at the backside of Astoria at the confluence of the Columbia River and Pacific Ocean. We stopped often for "rest stops" and to grab a few snacks, and then stopped in at the Crab Broiler near Seaside for a late lunch. From there, we traveled the back roads through Jewel, where a big elk feeding pasture is located. We also stopped at a one-room schoolhouse I had to take a gander at and use the bushes. When we dropped off Uncle Dwight and Toby that evening, Dwight said, "You guys are the eating-est and peeing-est bunch I ever saw." We still have a chuckle remembering his words.

DWIGHT WAS SEXY

God gave Dwight a boatload of testosterone. I know most folks would just whisper this facet to a few select family members, but people are what they are, and I have always strived to tell it like it was. I could provide several examples of Uncle Dwight's higher than normal T-power, but I think I'd better just say there were several other dalliances between Uncle and the ladies. He met some of the women at dances and others because they were neighbors, after Eva died. Women seemed attracted to Dwight for several reasons: He kept himself nice. He was enjoyable to be around. He was fit. He had money. Occasionally, I'd see jealousy develop between the ladies when they'd run into each other at get-togethers.

Dwight's first wife, Eva, died suddenly in her sleep in the fall of 1976 while they were visiting my sister Carol in La Grande. Eva was in her mid-seventies by then. Uncle Dwight and Aunt Eva had truly been mates, so her abrupt passing was difficult for him. The shock of finding his beloved one cold in their bed was difficult for him to accept and initially, he was quite emotionally unstable.

His next significant relationship was with the woman who had been helping take care of Grandpa and Grandma on the chicken farm for many years. Dwight's relationship with Toby was strong and durable. It lasted several years until she, too, passed away.

When Dwight was in his early eighties, he took up with a woman in her mid-thirties and soon they embarked on an extensive trip to New Zealand and Australia. Of course, Dwight footed the bill. If her teenage son had not taken a liking to Uncle's .38 pistol (which he stole), things might have become more serious. I helped resolve the May/December situation in an amiable manner.

DOING HIM IN

In a way, it was sex that did my Uncle Dwight in after he married for the second time. That union was to a woman I came to dislike with a passion, as Dwight eventually did too when her submerged personality gradually grew horns. It seems odd to me now, but before their wedding, they both came to Mom and me to get our blessing. As diplomatically and as firmly as possible, we both indicated the problems we foresaw. Perhaps we should have been more to the point, or maybe it was late-age crazy for Dwight and he was beyond help at that time.

Dwight's second wife came with the baggage of a worthless and lazy 45-year-old son who couldn't lick a postage stamp even on his good days. Dwight had to fix the son's crap car repeatedly because "The Baggage" would use only the emergency brake to slow and stop the vehicle, and abused the vehicle every way possible, causing innumerable other mechanical problems. Even worse, his wife was snitching cash that eventually rose to the tune of two thousand dollars *a month*, which she gave to her ne'er do well son. I know this fact because my wife, Joan, was keeping the books.

One time, Dwight's wife-creature bragged to Joan and I, and to our daughter, about "doing" every boy in her high school class. Of course, it wasn't a huge class—just 25 kids—but I strongly suspect she messed with the boys in the grade above and below as well. To cap it off, she'd already been "led" to the matrimonial alter three times before Uncle Dwight asked for her hand.

Well, after the honeymoon had worn itself thin, this wife's true colors were smoked out. She was truly a piece of work—not God's handiwork—but maybe even he has a bad day sometimes when hooking up chromosomes. It became abundantly clear that Dwight's wife was hitting him. Oh, I know he was bigger, and a man, but the dismal truth is this woman was shit-assed mean (as my mother would say).

It is my belief that there's a great amount of unreported "man beating" swept under the other piles of crap we endure in this sometimes nuts-so society. And which is worse—words or fists? They both leave wounds that hurt and scars that fester in the body or mind, often both. Dwight would have had an extremely hard time proving he was being hit because the woman was sneaky-slick— like many people of that ilk. And she'd undoubtedly had a lot of practice with previous victims.

I need to mention that this woman put great store in her meowing cats. Those felines were the center of her universe—as long as there was a Sugar Daddy Big Bucks like Dwight to care for them all. So naturally, I'd take my dog over there every once in a while just to get a little Irish ruckus going and hopefully raise her dander. Baiting the cats did not seem to worsen the situation for Dwight.

So what did my Uncle Dwight do? After seven years of marriage, he started pretending he was sick and would admit himself to the hospital, just to get away from her. The hospital couldn't keep him long, but he was thankful for the respite from her dismal rear end for the couple of weeks they'd let him stay.

One time while Dwight was a patient at the Hillsboro Hospital, the husband-beater arrived and put on a show of visiting him just as his heart doctor was leaving the room. She called out to Dwight in her overly loud voice, "Isn't he handsome, for a Jew?" My wife witnessed this unbelievable crudeness and was aghast.

Around that time, Uncle Dwight came and asked me what it would take to get a divorce, and I told him about the financial realities. His wife was entitled to half of his considerable estate. That was a grim day for Uncle.

I believe Uncle Dwight would have lived to be a 100 years old if this woman had not been his wife. Well, when he died at 96, she announced that she wanted to be buried with him, not with any of her three former husbands, or with her birth family. But Dwight had told me, in private, to make sure this did not happen. As executor of his and her will, I managed to ship her remains to a more "suitable" end place.

GOOD HEALTH, BAD HEALTH, AND KIDS

Dwight had a heart attack at the age of 53. He and his wife Eva, and Toby were in the Forest Grove High School football stadium at the time, watching my team play against Tigard during my junior year. Knowledge about heart attacks was still in the dark ages back then, but Uncle Dwight recovered.

Eighteen months later, he suffered another heart attack. At that point, his physician, Dr. A. V. Jackson (a man way ahead of his time) encouraged Dwight to modify his lifestyle. He took the doctor's advice to change his diet and dropped from 205 to 165 pounds. Dwight had always been active, which served him well. Luckily, he loved rhubarb and ate some just about every morning of his life thereafter. One medicine proscribed to him was the blood thinner, Warfarin (Coumadin), and he gave himself a shot in the stomach each morning with a very long, scary needle.

Dwight developed Type II diabetes in his late eighties. He and my mom were both nailed by this problem and they handled it in stellar fashion, figuring out for themselves that food management and increased exercise would help. This was way before the medical industry made the connection.

DWIGHT'S GIVING SIDE

Dwight was a Free Mason, which used to be a rather secretive organization, and often associated with the Shriners. The order is comprised of men who tend to be generous, community-spirited individuals. My dad, R. Glenn Ritchey, was a 32nd degree Mason, which is top of the heap, as well as a Shriner. I do not know how far my Grandpa Mac and Dwight progressed with the Free Masons, but Uncle Dwight and a fellow named Charlie Piper were instrumental in getting our granddaughter, Kristy Cline, into the Shriners Hospital in Portland. Jim Dorman and Harold Johnson were very helpful regarding the Mason's organization.

Kristy with Uncle Dwight, 1980

Kristy was born with a severe spinal defect that required numerous operations before she was even two years old. She is now in her thirties but confined to a wheelchair. My wife, Joan, and I raised her for nearly seven years.

Dwight looked for opportunities to help people of our community with their shop projects. Some of the folks he helped told me what Uncle Dwight had made for them—cabinets, shelves, and even items from his lathe. And boy, were they tickled. Uncle Dwight built my ten-foot-long workbench, patterned after the one in his shop. The top was constructed from kiln-dried fir, two-inch by six-inch tongue-and-groove with a three-quarter inch piece of seven-layer plywood. That bench was built like a tank and is still really stout, or *skookum.*

Dwight liked athletic endeavors, and so on Sundays he often initiated a game of softball or croquet, both of which were favorite family endeavors. He was a big fan of the Portland Trailblazers basketball team, and in 1977, the year they won the NBA Championship, we purchased a ticket for him. It was great fun for Joan and me to enjoy the game, the crowd, and especially him. And when he'd watch the games at home he'd yell and holler, and get so excited that he had to wear thick gloves to keep from chewing off his fingernails. That's just the way he lived everything in his life—to the fullest! *Everything* was always one-hundred-ten-percent with him!

DWIGHT'S IDIOSYNCRASIES

Uncle Dwight was a hearty eater, and I always thought he should have raised a few fat hogs because he loved pork and ham dinners so much. He never failed to show up when my wife was cooking Easter ham or, well, actually, any time we invited him over.

Dwight often ordered small wooden crates of corned beef from Argentina or Brazil, each holding 24 one-pound packages. Somehow, I've managed to retain fifteen or twenty of these neat, old wooden boxes with dovetailed joints. And somehow, Uncle Dwight's digestive system could handle great amounts of sodium—besides all the smoked foods, he'd pour the salt on at most meals.

Dwight, like his father, Mac McCue, enjoyed poetry and easily memorized lengthy poems. One particular favorite was about an outhouse, which he referred to as a "biffy." It turns out the origin of that word was Canadian and Upper Midwest slang. My dad was also good at memorization, and thankfully, some of their abilities transferred to me. My longest memorized poem was 'The Cremation of Sam McGee," and parts of it still pop into my Irish mind. Reciting poetry is a rather fun thing to do when driving through sparse country like Eastern Oregon, or just lying in bed waiting for sleep to come and take you away.

One trait Dwight shared with my mom is that they both talked to themselves when they were alone. A couple of times he was unaware that I was nearby and I answered the question he was posing to himself. He was surprised, but gave me a big smile.

And Dwight was truly a man of habit. He would count the dandelions as he dug them up—on his hands and knees—and often had 300-dandelion days (those were good days), even when he was way into his nineties. When the doctor recommended twenty-five repetitions of a certain exercise, and ten of another, Uncle Dwight would do them, period, without fail, for years. And every morning, he got on his stationary exercise bicycle for a serious workout. In some respects, he was like a machine with a soul.

For farm work clothes, Uncle Dwight wore J.C. Penney long sleeved blue shirts with two pockets, the same as I do in the summer. His overalls were the striped bib-style, and he wore ankle high work shoes for footwear. I never became partial to bibbies, but I can sure think of several advantages, which I have greatly exaggerated in the story, "I Love Pockets" that appears earlier in this book.

The Oregon Electric train went by twice a day, separating Dwight's house from the home of his parents. The train schedule was pretty regular, so Eva was usually out there to wave at the engineer and the guy in the red caboose. They all were on a first-name basis after a few seasons. My mom would catch that train when she headed to Portland for secretarial school on Mondays, then return on it every Friday evening, getting off at the Maple Street crossing. Occasionally railroad bums jumped off the sidecars to get a handout, but those were provided only after the bums did some farm work to earn a meal. There seemed to be more fairness all the way around in those Good Old Days. As for me, I used to try my balance and walk the steel rails, and hop from tie to tie as a boy. But those rails looked pretty rusty the last time I trekked out there; part of the line had been removed years ago. I think dismantling all those tracks was an unfortunate lack of foresight—rail freight costs remain the lowest for transportation of goods.

Uncle Dwight believed in God, tithed, prayed regularly, and was particularly close to the minister, Lloyd Uecker, for many, many years. Lloyd was the minister of the Forest Grove Methodist Church and led an interdenominational Bible study.

He also loved his garden and grew a lot of vegetables, berries, apples, and pears, and as a result did a lot of home canning and freezing. He had flowers, too, and always planted marigolds because they help keep the bugs at bay. One time the weekly Forest Grove *News Times* sent a reporter out to take a photo of his gigantic sunflowers, which, if I recall correctly, exceeded twelve feet high.

Dwight's Winter Squash, 1990

NEAR THE END

Uncle Dwight spoke at length on a great many subjects and I was almost always willing to "listen up" because he wasn't just flapping his jaws. I've managed to hold onto all of my uncle's photo albums and his boxes of snapshots. I also have several of his diaries—he jotted down items he found of interest in little notebooks for many years. I wish he'd been able to expand on some of the topics, but most of the notebooks were pre-printed diaries that provided scant room under each date.

I need to mention the time when Dwight was in his eighties and he took off for Hillsboro without his pants. Apparently, on the way, his truck developed a problem and he had to find a telephone booth to call for help, but he was dressed only in his BVDs. I sure wondered at the time how that could happen. But now that I'm close to eighty myself, I have a clear understanding.

Near the end of his life, Uncle Dwight offered to sell his beautiful farm to Joan and me for a price in excess of half a million dollars, but the purchase would have pushed us particularly hard financially. Looking back, I wish we had made the stab, but oh well. If we had purchased his property, most likely his house, barn, and shop would still be standing. I miss those homey Dwight McCue structures.

My Uncle Dwight was a joy to be around and I still miss that special, special relationship I had with him.

======

The following story is by my cousin, Doris Norman, who was Wilby's daughter. Doris taped Uncle Dwight while preparing a thorough family genealogy and I include an excerpt here that contains some poignant recollections of an earlier time.

Excerpt from interview of Dwight McCue

Dwight L. McCue interviewed by Doris Norman.

When I was a little boy, about three years old, my brothers built a small two-wheel cart and made a harness for our dog, Shep, so he could pull me around the place. We lived at the south end of Washington Street in New Ulm, Minnesota, with nothing but open spaces to the south. A cow herder grazed the city cows in vacant areas used as pasture during the day, but brought them back in the evening so they could be milked.

Well, one afternoon, I took off with Shep and headed out for the pasture. I didn't tell anyone where I was going. I fell asleep among the cows, or so they say. Mother was surely concerned about my whereabouts and had everyone looking for me. The herdsman found me and took me home. I don't remember if I got paddled, but I never forgot that escapade with the dog.

In 1909, I started school in our one-room schoolhouse, but they had to lock the door to keep me in there. I wanted to be home with Mother. That was the same year Merritt came down with the measles. Mother had him isolated at one end of the living room by hanging a sheet from the ceiling. Sister (my sister Margaret Helen) and I felt sorry for him being confined in that small area, so we would roll marbles back and forth under the sheet to help pass the time. Both Sister and I came down with the measles later. Poor Mother, she never had a dull moment.

In the fall of 1910, Orral ran away from home, refusing to complete his education. At that time, we were living at 1895 Waltham Street in St. Paul. Our folks were real concerned about Orral's whereabouts because they couldn't locate him for a year-and-a-half. It turned out that he was in Kansas, working in a button factory. Dad set out to get him and left on the train from the Merriam Park station. The rest of the family stood on the right-of-way and waved goodbye. Dad brought Orral back and found him a job at the Minnesota Transfer working in the roundhouse, located about five blocks from our home. Mother would fix him lunch and Sister and I were supposed to take it to him at noon. Well, one day we were on our way up the railroad track with the lunch pail when I started goofing off. I was swinging the lunch pail in a circle over my head. All of a sudden, the lid came open and the fried chicken rolled down the bank and got covered with cinders. We didn't know what to do. So, we picked up the pieces and took the pail back to Mother. She washed off the chicken as best she could and sent us back up the railroad tracks.

Merritt had a paper route when we lived on Waltham,

and he carried both the *Pioneer Press* and the *St. Paul Dispatch*. He had about 300 customers. On Saturdays, we would go around to those customers and pick up the old papers, bundle them, and sell them to Waldorf Paper Company. There was a crippled boy on his route that Merritt felt sorry for, so he bought the boy a wind-up train for Christmas. I'll never forget going with my brother to pick out the present, nor forget the expression on that little boy's face when he opened the gift. That sure was a real happy Christmas for all of us.

In the years before we had a car, Dad would hire a team and buggy, and we would go for Sunday afternoon jaunts. Those were always the highlights of our week. The drive would last for four or five hours. Dad was in his prime when he was driving a pair of spirited horses.

We got our first car in 1916. It was a four-cylinder Buick, an open car. By then, we'd moved to 317 South State Street in New Ulm. Mother and Dad had gone to the Twin Cities on business and our brother, Merritt, was doing some electrical work in Mankato on the high school. Sister and I thought it would be fun to drive over to see our brother, so we got some pillows to sit on so I could see over the steering wheel. We made it over to Mankato just fine, and found the high school and our brother, but we got a real cool reception from him, then he bawled us out for coming! Sister and I were so disappointed. Merritt drove us home that evening and told us to never try that again. I can't recall if we told the folks what we had done. Live and learn.

Most every Sunday afternoon during the summer months, the family would take a drive around the southern part of Minnesota. Merritt and Dad did most of the driving. On one particular Sunday, we were on our way to St. Cloud, with Merritt driving. Most of the time we sped along between 20 and 25 miles per hour, but this time, Merritt reached 50, the top speed of the car. Everyone held his breath as we watched the speedometer. It was a long time before I was allowed to drive that fast.

It was rare that we wouldn't have at least one flat tire during our drives. The tires were guaranteed for 3500 miles back then. I can remember the first 5000-mile tire, which was produced in the early 1920s. In the fall, we would jack up the car and take off the tires, wrap them in newspapers, and store them in the basement.

In 1922, the four of us—Mom, Dad, my sister, and I—left on a trip for the East Coast. We drove a 1919 Buick, six-cylinder open touring car. We camped along the way, and set up our 8-foot by 10-foot tent and folding cots each night. We cooked on a two-burner gas stove. We camped at country churches or schoolhouses, because those always had a handy source of water and outside "biffies." We didn't carry a road map, as there were no trails to follow.

Dad had a very good sense of direction so we depended on him to guide us. We made it through Chicago in good shape at a time when there was a cab strike going on. We ran into a terrible rainstorm while traveling around Lake Erie and had to stay in a fellow's barn for the night. Some days we didn't travel very far because the roads were impassable on account of rainstorms. I think we averaged about 140 miles per day. We stopped to see cousin George Taylor in Philadelphia, Pennsylvania, and Rose Dale in Springfield, Massachusetts. We drove through New York City and crossed the Hudson River to the New Jersey side. On our way home, we drove through the parts of Illinois and Indiana where Dad grew up. Most of the roads were gravel in the Eastern states, and dirt in the Middle West. The only tourist camp we stayed at was in Clinton, Iowa, on our way home. I don't remember how many miles we drove, but I think it was around 2,900 in all. The trip took three weeks.

In 1926, Dad, Mother, and I drove to the West Coast in a 1926 Buick sedan. We camped along the way and brought along better equipment for camping than we'd had on our trip East in 1922. The tent fastened to the side of the car, and we had cabinets built on the running boards to hold our camping gear. Sometimes we stayed at tourist camps, but they were few and far between. We followed the Yellowstone Trail part of the way, which made it easier to find our way, and stayed in Yellowstone Park for four days. The roads through North Dakota and Montana were just cow trails, two ruts to follow with grass in between. We stopped in Seattle to see the Newton family (Dwight later married Eva Newton), and in San Francisco to visit with cousin, Vera Bonham. We also spent a couple of days in Salt Lake City, and three days visiting relatives in Colorado.

SECTION 3

**Stories, Poems, and Excerpts
By My Family
Who Came Before**

Introduction To Section 3

The final section of this book contains poems and stories written by my family members, all of whom are deceased. The authors are from both my maternal and paternal sides.

The first two authors, Mr. W. Howard Hamm and Mr. Richard Ramsell, were my cousins and they both wrote mostly poetry. The third selection, excerpted from *Ever Westward*, is by my great uncle William C. Stucker (my grandmother's brother), who had a weekly news column in the Burlington, Iowa *Hawkeye Gazette*.

W. Howard Hamm

W. Howard Hamm's first poem is about a mustang stallion and I've included the two-page pencil sketch paired with it from his book, *Trail Dust*. A second poem by Mr. Hamm, "The Church in the Canyon," published in *Trail Dust 2*, follows with its accompanying drawing. Copies of his books can still be purchased through Trail Dust Books & Paintings, P.O. Box 26, Valley Falls, Kansas 66088.

Trail Dust
by W. Howard Hamm

Excerpt of Preface from *Trail Dust I*.

This collection of pen and ink drawings and poems is presented as a large-format book, 10.5-inches tall x 14-inches wide. The book was first printed in 1950, and then reprinted in 1981.

W. Howard Hamm attended the Kansas City Art Institute in the Dust Bowl days of the 1930s. From there, he went to Arizona where he fell in love with the desert and mountains of the west. And there he stayed. His work was shown in many cities of the west and he has painted decorative panels in business houses and homes. The largest and best known is a 520-square-foot mural in the Kendall State Bank in Valley Falls, Kansas.

Excerpt from Preface of *Trail Dust II*

Trail Dust II is a collection of drawings 'nd notes that cover many miles of trails in the Southwest country... This new *Trail Dust* is even larger than the first volume and, we feel, quite interesting. Each plate may be removed from the booklet for framing. We have attempted to glean the grain from the chaff, and hope we have achieved our purpose. The saddle is back in the tack room and the shoes are pulled from Old Red, and he is turned out to pasture.

We have compiled this collection in the hope that the poems and illustrations may be enjoyed by others traveling the same trails. May we wish you a pleasant journey.

Adios Amigos.

I would like to dedicate this book to my daughter, Alondra Kay.

W. Howard Hamm

Tucson, Arizona

The Mystery Mustang (A Legend)
by W. Howard Hamm

He lived above the canyon rim—
Above the sage and sand—
This mystery stallion of the range,
The king of the wild-horse band.

When he stopped at a new-made water hole
High in a mountain gap
A waiting puncher tossed his rope—
He had walked straight into the trap.

He shook his head. His ears laid back.
Then he wheeled as he started his run.
The puncher yelled when he hit the rope—
But the horse, again, had won!

Screaming once, the mustang whirled
And with flying mane was gone.
The rider watched him up the trail
And sadly waved him on.

"TH' MYSTERY MUSTANG"

Th' Church In Th' Canyon
by W. Howard Hamm

Th' church up in th' canyon...
is there for you—'nd me.
Th' rancher or th' ranch hand...
Th' cowboy on his knee...

It isn't made of marble ...
Th' seats are merely chairs,
'nd, folks that go t'meeting here
they don't put on airs.

Some of us don't get to church...
But—we're like all th' rest.
It stands there as a symbol...
in th' buildin' of th' west.

Richard Ramsell

Next, I've included the Preface from Richard Ramsell's book, *The View From Where I Stand,* and one of his poems, "Preparations," which refers to making wine, something I also do—in abundance—so I simply could not resist. Wine is a warming friend, as he states so well.

The View From Where I Stand
by Richard Ramsell

From Preface

As far back as I can remember I have been interested in life around me. Expeditions to the lake, riding along while my father looked for pheasants, and our first trip to the Black Hills of South Dakota were big deals. With one of us three boys in the front seat of the Model T touring car with my father, and the other two boys on either side of my mother in the rear, we scoured the roads around our hometown of Huron. Lucky indeed were those birds that escaped our scrutiny. We vied to see who saw the most birds.

I learned to associate sporting people with the natural scene, and I formed an appreciation of both. From this interest, I thought of nature and social activity together and found humor in it. After reaching the age of 50, and not being satisfied in what I was doing, I went back to school and finished work on a degree that enabled me to become a librarian in an elementary school. There, I had requests for many poems for holidays and various activities. I used what was available for a time, but soon found myself repeating the same ones. In time, I found it easier to write a new one than to find a poem that hadn't already been used many times. These I supplied to the students and teachers and they enjoyed them. The practice became habitual and numerous people have asked me to put some of them in a book. In *The View From Where I Stand*, I collected some of them. I hope readers enjoy reading them as much as I enjoyed writing them.

Richard L. Ramsell

Preparations
by Richard Ramsell

Each Christmas I make cookies
With which to spread some cheer
They seem to be quite popular
At that time of year.

Comes spring, I pick some rhubarb,
The jam I make is fine
But I am better known by far
For making rhubarb wine.

For wine is an elixir
To palate and to sight,
A warming friend at hard day's end
When you get home at night.

William (Bill) C. Stucker

William (Bill) C. Stucker was born in 1885. He listened carefully when his father, George Stucker, a captain in the Civil War, talked about war incidents with his close friends — other men who had survived that terrible uncivil tragedy. One of his father's best friends, J. M. Virgin, married Bill's sister, Susan, and kept a diary on Sherman's March to the sea.

Bill Stucker's book, *Ever Westward*, is a fictional presentation of our combined families' never-ending westward trek. One branch has resided in Hawaii for nearly fifty years, and now we have a Samoan connection.

Bill Stucker was the only one of those three relatives I was fortunate enough to meet. He lived to be 99-and-a-half-years old. Uncle Bill made his living by farming. His home near Pleasant Grove, Iowa, is now occupied by his granddaughter, Claudia, and her husband, Mike Hoelzen. Semi-annual family reunions are held there each July and at the end of the next one, we will open — with much anticipation — a twenty-year-old time capsule stored in the family farm's root cellar. Each family "twig" had the opportunity to write down a few words for posterity two decades ago.

Ever Westward
by Bill Stucker

From Preface.

Ever Westward is a result of being retired and having time to let thoughts roam back to youthful days when, as a small boy, I was privileged to listen to stories and incidents of the early settlement of our fair state by those who had a part in it. Most especially do I recall sitting fascinated and spellbound as I heard old Civil War veterans (one of whom was my father) as they lived again in memory those exciting and tragic days.

In the present age when pioneering is upward instead of westward, and the youth of our land are thinking of rockets and missiles and planning trips to the moon and other planets, it is interesting to remember that little more than a century ago, their great-grandfathers were making their way across the continent in covered wagons pulled by oxen, a drama I have tried to picture in this book.

Although I confess to having done some research and checked with some reliable historical records, I make no claim for the historical worth of *Ever Westward*. Only as memory serves have these lines been written. The characters and families in this book, except those of national fame and renown, for the most part are fictitious; and the events—other than battles, movements of troops, and the surrender of military strongholds—are imaginary.

Ireland—I Got Lucky!

I got lucky, and then I got more of that famous Irish luck in the fall of 2014. I, meaning Joan and me, headed for Ireland!

A portion of that Emerald Island is hauntingly beautiful, some of it stark and bare, but *all* the folks are friendly. Our small tour bus of twelve individuals was led by Danny O'Flaherty, who sang to us every day and every evening in both Gaelic and English. Plus he led us on six unscheduled interesting and wonderful stops, some lasting for a half day. Our group was squired around by a very able and funny Michael Rooney, who had a never-ending supply of Murphy jokes.

With the help of our guides, I walked where my ancestors had hailed from, near the town of Bushmills in Northern Ireland. The story goes that the family branches of Nichols and Moores left Ireland in the winter of the big Potato Famine in 1848, and traveled to America on one of those infamous coffin ships. More than a third of the passengers on those boats died at sea and the remainder almost died in America's slums before finding work.

Roger in Ireland with two dummies, like the one in the middle

RIVER BUSH
STRANOCUM BRIDGE

My ancestors survived the daunting odds and our extended family is still trekking on.

I even brought a bit of an Irish peat bog home to Oregon, rather than a cloverleaf. Danny O'Flaherty spoke at length in Gaelic with a lady who said she was still burning peat in her home. Each dried piece of bog looks like a giant horse turd.

Danny O'Flaherty and an Irish lady examining dried peat piles, 2014

A common Gaelic sign on the roads when leaving Irish towns state, *Slán Go Foil.* Which means—*Goodbye For Now!*

Acknowledgements

Again, my biggest helper on this, my second book of mostly short stories, was my wife Joan Marie Michalke Ritchey. She *always* gives one hundred and ten percent like my uncle Dwight. I also thank Mary Jane Nordgren, Mary Slocum, and Joe Schrader who are always willing to help and offer suggestions. In addition, I have been greatly encouraged by many readers of my first book, *Hankering For The Way It Was*. It is neat to see your very first attempt at scribbling being passed from reader to reader. I hear about the laughs, the memories relived and relating to life as we lived it back in those older days.

I also want to thank a good friend and former appraisal colleague, John R. Claassen, who assisted with some of the artwork.

About The Author

I started writing stories when I was nearly 70 years old and now I've reached three-quarters of a century, speeding right ahead towards 80. One of my long time friends mentioned a possible similarity to Grandma Moses, but I think perhaps not....

Thankfully, most days I don't feel like a grandpa and for sure not a great-grandpa, which has happened eight times already. Hopefully, I'll be like one of those rare wines that actually get better with age. I figured out that I'm allowed to lie a little bit more now—well, there are fewer interruptions when you are laying the foundation for a bunch of BS. And maybe that is what old age is—a valid license to fabricate.

Index Of Names